BEARS
IN THE
RAW

Paul D. Cain/Luke Mauerman

Cain, Paul D. and Mauerman, Luke
Bears In The Raw

First Edition
Library of Congress Control Number: 2018965354

ISBN 978-1-7324567-2-3 (paperback)

Published by

AquaZebra™
Book Publishing

Cathedral City, California
www.aquazebra.com

Cover/interior design
Mark E. Anderson

AquaZebra™
Web, Book & Print Design
www.aquazebra.com

Printed in the United States of America

Foreword by Paul D. Cain

Never underestimate the power of a good conversation with a casual acquaintance.

So I've known Luke for several years, but very casually. He was the frequent companion of my artist friend George, with whom I sang in the Palm Springs Gay Men's Chorus for a couple of seasons (and who is so sexy it hurts). Not much of a talker. A deep, quiet guy. (When they don't talk much, you assume they're either deep or dumb. I knew Luke wasn't dumb—too much going on behind those glasses.)

Anyway, I was at a (naked) pool party during the summer of 2017. I went over to say "hey" to George, and got to talking with Luke. Somehow we got on the topic of writing. I told Luke that I had written a book, which not a lot of people in Palm Springs know. (I've lived in greater Palm Springs for seven years now, and my having written a book doesn't seem to interest anyone much. It was published when I lived and wrote columns for a few magazines in Reno, and I worked on it for years when I lived in Phoenix, so folks there knew and cared more. Here, it's kind of old news.)

Luke told me he had been a writer, so that pricked up my ears. I found out he had written for *BEAR* Magazine. Whoa! I loved *BEAR*! When I came out as gay at age 23 in 1984, there was nothing remotely like it that I ever found. Men in magazine porn were very young, mostly hairless, and usually hung like proverbial horses. I did not much like young people, even (especially) when I was young myself. And the aesthetic didn't really appeal to me—OK, the well-hung part was fine—but I liked bigger, hairier men. You know, men who looked like MEN, not boys. But you couldn't really miss or lament what you couldn't see. When I saw my first copy of *BEAR*, I was damn near thunderstruck! THESE were the kinds of guys I lusted after. They weren't necessarily fat, or always hairy, but it was clear that they weren't trying to conform to anyone else's idea of beauty. These were men who dared to look different—like MEN. I couldn't get enough—I don't remember if I bought a subscription, but I surely picked up a copy every month at our local gay bookstore. (Once upon a time—back in the 1980s and 1990s—large and mid-sized cities had local gay bookstores where you could purchase gay books and magazines that Barnes & Noble wouldn't carry. They also carried "smut," to make sure they could continue to keep the lights on. These also often served as gay community centers, and I miss them terribly—not just as a writer, but as an inveterate reader.)

Sorry—I digress.

Armed with Luke's information, I went into my box of porn to find my old *BEAR* magazines—I had just culled my stash earlier that summer, but hadn't gotten to the *BEAR* magazines. Good thing. I found some of Luke's articles (I also found some of the *100% Beef* magazines I had saved). I had dim memories of reading them—I was busy trying to get to the photos—but I loved Luke's writing. It was real, and raw. And he clearly loved and wanted to nurture the same community I did.

At the pool party, Luke had lamented losing his opportunity to have a writing outlet. I, too, hadn't had a writing outlet since 2008, after writing monthly columns for years. Luke was writing very specifically for a subset of the gay men's community—I was writing for a broader LGBT community in northern Nevada. Luke was more raw in his expression than I was, but I worked hard to be as transparent and honest as I could. So I thought, "What if we brought our collective work out of mothballs, and turned it into a book? Not only would it give US pleasure, it would also be a nice time capsule to see what two gay nudist bears were writing about in the 1990s and 2000s." I contacted another casual friend, Mark Anderson, who I knew was a local book publisher. We met with Mark, told him our idea, and *voila*! So Luke and I each had to find our previous work, obtain permissions from prior publishers, and determine which of our works stood the test of time to make an interesting book. And that's what you hold in your hand, dear reader.

We hope you like what we had to say—and how we said it—all those years ago. Perhaps this will jump-start our writing "careers" (at least Luke made a living from his writing; I seldom made a dime, but I had the freedom to write about anything that struck my fancy). But at this point, this is purely for fun, and to entertain an audience.

Foreword by Luke Mauerman

Twenty-two years ago, when I started writing my columns, I had no right to think these words would ever see the light of day again: You write them, they get put in a dirty magazine, and wind up in a bin somewhere. While people tended to keep their copies of BEAR Magazine for years, eventually everything non-digital gets tossed out.

So this has been an interesting experience in time travel, going through all my old columns two decades later.

They were never meant to be read as a single piece; I'm very aware of the repetitive nature they present.

And I was surprised at how much sex I wrote about; in real life, that's not me at all. I certainly did have my fair share, but, unlike my writing persona, I never kiss and tell—in fact, I loathe those who do. So it's an interesting little schism I've got going on. It was, after all, a smut magazine, and I was playing the part. Hopefully it makes for good reading.

My involvement with BEAR Magazine, which spawned my writing in the first place, was a freak accident, one of the most remarkable bits of good fortune ever to land in my lap.

BEAR Magazine: We can all recount the tale, we can recite it like A Christmas Carol: In 1987, a pair of edgy guys in San Francisco started a badly-Xeroxed pamphlet called

BEAR. Black and white print, half-size, saddle fold, and full of overly skinny or overly weighty men—but refreshingly non-conformist. Masculine men with facial hair. Nasty references to man sex and man buttholes.

It ... grew.

In August 1990, I had just moved to San Francisco. On my very first day in my new city, I went to the offices of this *BEAR* Magazine. It was in an old Mission District firehouse. I went, heart pounding in my chest, to buy a copy of the latest issue—and to buy a dirty video, too. I was scared to be there. But I made a joke with the hippie guy behind the counter about needing extra income. Did they ever hire help?

I was kidding. Mostly.

But I did get hired. Was so sure it wouldn't be right for me, it was so edgy and strange that I made an extra copy of the office keys just to keep as a souvenir from "those two-odd weeks in 1990 when I actually *worked* at BEAR!"

I still have those keys. And I spent five years working there. It remains the headiest time of my life. New to San Francisco, new to porn, always within sniffing distance of the sexiest men you could ever imagine. I was the prissy preppy-looking guy in the corner. I look at pictures of me back then and cringe—I SO didn't fit in. The people around me were on a lot of heavy drugs or dying of AIDS. Or both. I took refuge in the job itself, working late into the night, alone in the creaky old firehouse amid all your uncashed checks for Butthole Banquet II.

I don't think there was any aspect of the magazine I didn't do myself at one time or another. I paid its taxes. Swept its floors. Handled angry phone calls from people who didn't like the dildo they bought, and who failed to understand why they couldn't simply return it. Wrote some things, took some pictures, even held the video camera once. I was in charge of the mountain of published personal ads, a huge part of the magazine. Once a guy included his Prodigy handle—some kind of PXR99234@Prodigy.com as a way to contact him—and I remember thinking "sheesh ... what a geek."

The part I enjoyed the most was actually laying out the magazine, using Quark Xpress on a Mac LC-III. I sucked at it! *BEAR* Magazine, when I assembled it in 1994, looked its absolute worst. I didn't know what I was doing, so I just crammed everything onto each page, and then went on to the next. I kept using the wrong printing terms, but our printers never corrected me; they just knew what I meant and glossed over my mistakes without raising a fuss.

But it was fun.

We took care of our models. They were honored guests. We didn't pay them jack shit, but to this day, I'm still in touch with many.

Straight people have heard of *BEAR* Magazine. One night they made fun of it on Saturday Night Live, with John Goodman on the cover. I nearly fell off the couch yelling at the TV in shock.

Richard Bulger, the magazine's creator, sold it and moved away in 1994. I lasted a year under the new owner, but I was working two jobs and had been burning the candle at both ends of my life for too long. I couldn't keep going. Plus, the magazine started to change. It got corporate and weird. So I bailed. Walked away from being a part of this baby I'd helped nurse for half a decade. It wasn't easy for me to let go, but I always knew I'd have to at some point.

They let me keep a column, my own little page in my precious magazine. It was a perfect send-off. I had a quiet little perch to muse and navel-gaze, taking over from the previous columnist, the amazing John Dibelka.

The guy who bought *BEAR* in 1994 eventually ran the place into the ground, as homosexuals will do. *BEAR* shut its doors amid IRS tax seizures and more ill-will than you can shake a stick at. The name and brand have been revived by Wolfe Thompson and Teddy Roberts of Las Vegas. It publishes mainly online now, and has thousands of followers on Facebook.

When Scott McGillivray started *100% Beef* Magazine, I was delighted to continue my column for them, which I did until that magazine's demise in 2008.

Since then I haven't had a place to write, so I don't. Life moves on.

I've taken the liberty of writing one last column, years later, just to enjoy writing again and to recap my own journey. I hope you'll forgive the indulgence—my one last involvement with ghosts of the past.

Dedication by Paul D. Cain

For the Love of My Life, Kurt Jacobowitz-Cain

And nobody, but NOBODY, thought it would last!
Twenty-nine years and counting!

Dedication by
Luke Mauerman

For Richard Bulger

I'm very sorry you're dead, Honey

Acknowledgments by Paul D. Cain

Thanks to my friends who allowed me to write for a gay (now LGBT) audience, most especially Robrt Pela in Phoenix, the late, great Jack Nichols for *Gay Today.com*, the guys at *QBliss. net*, and Dennis Little in Reno, who gave me free rein for years in *Reno-Tahoe Outlands* and *Outlands* magazines. Thank you to all of my teachers, whether in or out of school. Thanks to the great folks at Scarecrow Press for publishing *Leading the Parade*. Thanks to my readers in Reno; my brothers in song in gay men's choruses in Los Angeles, Phoenix, Reno, and Palm Springs; and my many nudist and bear brothers everywhere.

Acknowledgments by Luke Mauerman

Many thanks to Wolfe Thompson and Teddy Roberts, current owners of *BEAR* Magazine, for allowing my old columns to see daylight once again. Same goes to Scott McGillivray and Larry Woolwine of *100% Beef* Magazine. To Rich Iremonger, Mike Benda, and Alec Wagner, who showed me what it's like to publish as a grown-up, and to Joseph Bean, who recommended personal essay writing to me in the first place. My deepest acknowledgement goes to Richard Bulger, founder of *BEAR* Magazine and best friend for those first few formative years. He, literally, taught me everything he knew.

Contents

Internet

It's a scary enough world already out there. But we just gotta go and make it that much worse, don't we?

We could just sit at home and watch TV, or take up a nice safe hobby like skydiving. But no. Sooner or later there comes a time when the heavens conspire agin' us and we can no longer find a dialectical path of reason for ourselves.

Sometimes, we just gotta get laid.

I know. You're more sensitive than that. You want to know what's on the inside of a man's heart first. Develop a strong, caring trust. A bond. And dick size doesn't matter, of course; we're more mature than that.

Or maybe you're just the quiet type; you already got a fella, you're a homebody and this magazine is hidden in your bottom drawer so your lover won't find it and, frankly, I'm gonna call your house and tell him if you don't send me money.

Whoever you are, I know you're grown up enough not to be insulted by what I'm talking about.

Sometimes you just gotta wrap yourself around a gritty, nasty, no-questions-asked, I-don't-give-a-shit-what-your-name-is, Christ-I-hope-I-never-see-you-again SEX ACT. The kind that puts your heart rate through the roof and leaves your knees all wobbly. The kind that, next day, you bend over to get a pan out of the bottom cupboard and your muscles are sore and you go, wait, I haven't been to the gym in a while—then you remember.

And you feel ashamed.

Yeah. That's the kind I'm talking about.

If you're not too particular about what might get stuck to the bottom of your boots, you can "go to the wall." That's what I call the peepshows—the flashy, sagging bits of the Las Vegas strip in nearly every town in America. Just don't look at what's attached to that dick poking through the hole in the wall of your little cubicle-with-broken-video-monitor. And for God's sake, don't sit down on anything. Just make sure the mouth beckoning through the hole is bearded. Stick yer meat in and hope for the best. Hope he doesn't bite.

But that's unsanitary. The attendants scowl an awful lot, and besides, you might be seen. Or arrested.

So now, we have the Shiny New Improved Internet. Being trashy just got technical—and a whole lot less messy.

You wanna get laid now, you gotta learn that JAVA doesn't mean Jism And Verbal Abuse. That a URL won't make your dick all drippy and sore. That IRC is good and ISDN is expensive. Now you can view the merchandise first, confirm your interests before sticking anything out that you might want to keep.

But it doesn't matter. We're all doomed anyway. Because at some point, you gotta go meet the guy.

Here you are, all horned out, got a raging hardon all the way over to his apartment, wondering what you're still doing up at 11:30 on a Tuesday night. You pack your condoms and cockring and your best hopes and suddenly you're there and you've already hit the buzzer.

He opens his door.

And he looks like an agéd bug.

Remember, it's what's on the *inside* that counts. That's what you keep telling yourself as, against your better judgment, you go into his dwelling. You wonder just whose picture that was he showed you online, 'cause it sure as shit isn't the creature that's inviting you to have a Diet Pepsi right now. Meanwhile, he hasn't cleaned the place since they came in to install the cable, and that was when it cost eight bucks a month. You scramble for clues as to whether he's an axe murderer. You wonder if you're going to get yourself outta this without having him go postal on you. Maybe, if you just hold yer nose and do him, it'll feel good. It'll reset your clock and you promise that tomorrow you'll take up jogging instead.

I tell ya, it's not easy being green.

Ya clicks your mouse, ya takes your chances.

I thought all this technology would make it easier to fuck. Got the voicemail, got the modem, got the great looks (shut up); yet making it all flow smoothly is elusive at best.

People don't actually lie. It's just that, if you have 35 years of pictures taken of you, which one would you post to entice horny visitors? Does it involve lighting that can't be found in nature?

You probably already know about the inverse corollary of getting laid: The more you want it, the harder it is to get. It's like they can smell your raging hormones, even at 2400 baud. And they stay away.

"You have no mail." Why doesn't it just say: "Nobody likes you. Get real."

Well, the opposite happens, too. All your chatting and picture swapping and hard work pays off, your inbox finally gets full of pert little promises and phone numbers—only then, you're not in the mood. You're a being of light that week, above the sins of the flesh. You wouldn't cross the street for anyone less than Dan Haggerty in a buckskin jockstrap bearing a wedding ring. So you can't keep up with the electronic invites that finally come in; your pals from the Internet get huffy. They say you're being a flake. Or a tease. And thus, once more, "You have no mail;" you're back at square one.

By which time you're horny again.

All this doesn't stop me. I'm an Internet Geek, through and through. I check for e-mail more than I scratch my balls, and considering where my balls have been lately, this is a bad thing.

I know that, when the planets line up just right, it can work out like a house afire.

That's why I keep coming back for more.

Luke

Surviving Failure

When I failed my first audition to become a casino dealer recently, it caused me to look back at a lot of my life's failures. I failed my driving test the first time. I still remember the only "F" I received in my academic career (on a math quiz in eighth grade) more than any "A" I ever received. My grades in law school were so bad after one semester that I withdrew rather than subject myself to any more humiliation. I was fired from a job after six weeks (after they kissed my butt to hire me).

I'm intimately acquainted with failure. It's a drag. It calls your entire sense of self-worth into question, and it robs you of self-esteem.

I've had my relationship failures, too. I came out in college at age 23, and for the next two years, I was so desperate to be in a relationship that it thwarted any chance I might have had of developing a healthy one. After two years of this frustration, just before graduation I met a man who lived in Phoenix through an *Advocate* personals ad, and I left Southern California to move in with him. After three weeks I knew we were in for a rocky ride, but so many friends had counseled me not to move that I felt I had to prove they were wrong. In many ways it wasn't a bad relationship, but after three years together I felt I couldn't continue any longer. Another failure.

I wonder if many of us don't feel that being GLBT is in and of itself some kind of failure. I know that before I came out, I wanted desperately to be "normal," not "different." Only as I grew to accept myself as I am, not as I felt I was supposed to be, did I began to appreciate the benefits of being different. We "different" folks can see the world both in the "normal" way (growing up in a "normal" society and with "normal" friends and relatives), and in a "different" way (understanding the marginalized, the outcasts, the peculiar). (As Martha Stewart says, that's a good thing.) In my experience, this usually gives us a heightened level of compassion for others. Unless they successfully challenge their assumptions of superiority, straight wealthy WASP (White Anglo Saxon Protestant) men often appear compassion-impaired in comparison to us. (Exhibit A: George W. Bush.) My "differentness," which I shunned so fiercely as a child, is probably the greatest blessing God gave me.

Having listed all my failures, I've had some successes, too. I did pass my driving test on the second try (as Dustin Hoffman said in *Rain Man*, "I'm an excellent driver"). I graduated as valedictorian of my college. I took the remaining money I had saved toward law school, and used it to buy a house. I spent five years on my last job in Phoenix before my husband and I moved to Reno. Kurt and I just celebrated twelve wonderful years together. And I'm **going** to become a dealer—it's just a matter of time and patience. Sometimes failure is the best thing that can happen to you.

Paul

Kiss

The lights are dark. A sultry CD's playing in the corner, probably *Enigma,* or them *Deep Forest* guys. You sit with your fella, the one you just found, on the couch. No. Wait. The bed. Things are going even better than you'd planned. You're sitting on the bed. A shaggy, gorgeous face leans your way. He's gonna kiss you. That smell—the one of spit and beer and of just plain guy—wafts your way; you can almost taste it; you're ready and ...

WHAM!!

What you expect to be a sensuous, lingering, romantic moment turns instead into an assault of saliva—significantly thicker and cooler than your own. In 0.8 seconds you've been to his tonsils and back. His uvula tastes fine. The secrets of his mouth and dentistry are revealed. No suspense, no surprises, and it's over—you've only got his dick to work on now.

As a species, humans may be forgetting how to kiss.

Now don't go thinking I'm grinding an axe against a bad kisser I know somewhere. No, Jim Bennet, of 1188 Buchanan Street, San Francisco, California, this isn't about you, at least not *per se*. No targets. I don't kiss and tell. And I hereby absolve all my exes—both of them—of any bad kissing.

I just think that we're forgetting the value of a good kiss and that it's a harbinger of the decline of Western Civilization, that's all. Maybe someday people are even going to forget how to get fucked. And if that happens, I'll totally drop out of life—maybe even lose my aspirations to become a priest.

We know we're already forgetting how to write things down by hand. We sit back and let the machines do it. Sex comes direct via satellite and we don't lift a finger but to wipe up the cum. We know, too, that our lips still get plenty of exercise. We flap 'em a lot, slobbering out slings and arrows. Unwashed mouths blare words, insults.

Whatever happened to finesse with those lips? A tickle. An idea. Driving someone wild?

As far as actual kissing technique, it's up to you. Ya gotta be original. If you're kissing me, I'd like it if there were actually lips involved: A wet, waggling pylon of dripping tongue definitely has a place on my personal morphology—including the mouth as things progress. But for me, a kiss starts with the lips. If you think your intended's lips are skanky, then maybe you need to reconsider the whole thing anyway.

In almost any sizeable city you can suck a stranger's dick and never see his face. Ever done that? What's more, ever done that, gone home, and jerked off again while thinking about something else? It's OK. No one here would ever take that away from you, or say you're a bad person for doing it. We all need it once in a while, and come home with dirt over the knees of our Levi's. The body-sex clock is reset and we feel pretty much OK again.

This column is about the other kind. When you get a chance to take your time, create a little magic and a little suspense. Do you still go at it like you're in a hurry? Like if you don't get things started soon you'll have to put another quarter in the slot?

There's a whole world of senses that we're trained to ignore. One thing I've learned is when you really want to make a point, back off and don't. You'll drive 'em wild.

I had a music professor taught me something that really stuck with me. She sat at a huge concert grand piano in an empty studio and, poking with one finger, played the sounds of *do re mi fa sol la ti* ... She didn't play the last note, *do*. Never did. That was in 1983, and when I think about it I realize I'm still waiting for that goddamn note to happen. The expectation hung in the air of that echoing room and we found ourselves wanting to yell, "Oh, baby yeah! Finish me off!"

There's power in breaking the rules. Taking a wrong turn. Fucking with 'em a little. Next time you have a set of gums headed your way, do the unexpected: Take your time. Don't do something. That's right. Don't. Take the plunge—not. Be breathless. It's my favorite word. The tonsils and purple bumps at the bottom of your fella's tongue will still be there waiting for you. Only maybe he'll be a little breathless by the time you get there.

It's kind of a known thing that the most erotic pictures aren't necessarily those where a fat dick stretches a gaping butthole with grease and ooze. The erotic ones are where the person looking has to do some work on his own, in his mind. The possibilities of the unfinished. *BEAR* Magazine is erotic. We figure we whet the appetite, but that you have to do the rest of it yourself. It's part of the reason we're still in black-and-white. When we're replaced by a futuristic holodeck complete with moans and smells and slippery mucosa, do you think you'll ever need to leave the house again?

I love a good kiss. They're out there to be had, if you know where to get 'em. And I've been told I'm a good kisser. Not that it matters now—I'm totally aware I'll never get kissed again, after writing shit like this in front of God and everybody. Oh, well. It was fun while it lasted.

Luke

Coming Out (More): Your Choice

I came out in 1984, at the ripe old age of 23. (I'm listed in the credits as a technical adviser for the 1980s movie "The Last American Virgin.") While some people edge their way out of the closet, I broke off the hinges. I had been piecing things together for several years, but once I learned to reconcile my spirituality with my sexuality, I came out proudly and never looked back.

So why did I come out? My mother instilled in me the importance of telling the truth, and I didn't want to live with the emotional dissonance of lying to the world every day, even if by omission (or cleverly changing pronouns). (Ironically, Mother was not pleased about my disclosure, but over the years she has learned to accept what she cannot understand with reasonable grace.) And since I wanted to find a lover, I neither wanted my search to be furtive, nor did I want to be so "discreet" as to be rendered invisible.

Should *you* come out? Pragmatist that I am, I believe the benefits outweigh the disadvantages. While I'm sure I haven't gotten some jobs because I'm openly gay, I wouldn't enjoy working with/ for homophobes. And while I lost some friends as a result, my honesty has probably made me more good friends than it ever would have cost me. (Realize, too, that most people are dealing with their own issues, and *your* sexuality seldom is one of them.

Conversely, other people often know things about you that you don't tell them, in which case your not coming out may make you appear ashamed of your sexuality, whether you are or not.)

For lesbians and gay men, being "out" is usually a matter of degree. First, you must be "out" to yourself; that is, you must recognize your own primary same-sex attraction. The next steps come in different order for different people (some may never come, which is OK too):

- You learn not to fight your sexual orientation (for example, by dating or marrying someone of the opposite sex)
- You begin to reveal your orientation to others, usually co-workers, friends, and family (although some people feel more comfortable doing so first with relative strangers)
- You may begin to experience affectional/sexual expression with another who is similarly inclined (while optional, I highly encourage this step!)
- You may develop a serious relationship with someone of the same sex
- You may desire a group (or groups) of like-minded friends, perhaps sharing common hobbies or interests
- You may wear jewelry or clothing that identifies your sexual orientation
- You may participate in gay parades and festivals
- Ultimately, you might even become comfortable enough to discuss your experiences as a gay person with the media, perhaps in your local newspaper or on TV. (Or maybe you'll write a column for a magazine that serves your local gay/lesbian community, as I do.)

While there is no "right" way to be gay, can you identify where you are in the process? Feeling free to be who you are without apology or shame in any situation is a precious gift you can give yourself. Not only that, you can serve as an example to counter the stereotypes and lies about gay people. (You also get to show straight people how tolerant they are, which can be a lot of fun!)

The motto for National Coming Out Day (every October 11) is "Take your next step," a wonderfully practical approach. If you can identify a way in which you would like to become more personally liberated (following my friend Rita Mae Brown's belief that "you are as sick as you are secret"), then that becomes *your* next step in coming out. (As for me, I've been *so* out for *so* long that there really are no further steps I can even conceive. I suppose I could buy a T-shirt that says, "*Everybody* knows I'm gay," but it would be redundant.)

I didn't have any choice about being gay, but I did have a choice about what kind of gay person I would be. I've chosen to be open and honest, and I've never regretted it. Since coming out, I have lived my life by the statement of Andre Gide: "I would rather be hated for what I am than loved for what I am not." (Armistead Maupin's 1984 *Advocate* article, "Design for Living," helped, too.)

For 2002, you can give the gift of honesty to those you love. And for those of us who are *way* out, we would love to have the pleasure of your company on the front lines! Give some thought to what *your* next step might be, weigh the pros and cons, and I hope you'll join me in creating a world where sexual orientation is as value-neutral as left-handedness. May the New Year bring you all good things.

Paul

Seatbelts Please

I was born a poor white trash child, living in the shadow of Seattle's Boeing factory boom during the 1960s. A kid in a suburb doesn't have much of a shot at getting good validation for his desire to fuck other men. Those thoughts of man-to-man closeness creep up pretty early in life, don't they? I was well established in my kindergarten year by the time I knew that men were sexy and women weren't.

The maleness that set my heart to racing usually had a beard involved. Or at least a mustache. Body hair; a little extra around the middle of a man's belly; I used to ache over the image of President Grant on the 50-dollar bill my mom showed me.

How does a kid, with no knowledge of sex, get hooked on images of Teddy Roosevelt, Ernest Hemingway, and that Jason guy on *Here Come the Brides*? On Mr. French on *A Family Affair*? What IS that? What works its way into our little heads, reassuring us that one day we'll wake up to a bearded, bad-breath'd, blanket-hogging sonofabitch anyway?

But when puberty hits, and you get to put your hand deeper into the cookie jar of life, you learn to keep your mouth shut—damn quick. And your dream fades when you're taught that, if you're gonna "be one of those," you better learn to like show tunes.

The first dirty magazine I ever bought was *Blueboy*. I was in such a hurry to pluck it from the bookstore shelf unnoticed that I banged my head on an upper rack—all attention turned to me as I was littered with copies of *Sunset* and *Car and Driver*. A salesperson had to come over and reaffix the shelf, and to help restack all those magazines. Yet my reward when I got home? Pictures of blond skinny surfer boys. Young, pimply, hairless and looking like undercooked chicken. Was that the only option?

Yet in that *Blueboy* was one lone photo of gay porn legend Al Parker—it was an ad for an adult VHS video, available via mail order for $60.

I saw his beard and natural, sexy smile, and I knew things would be all right. There was hope after all. And maybe magazines could be pretty cool sometimes.

I spent five and a half years working at *BEAR* Magazine in San Francisco. Sure surprised the hell out of me ... it wasn't something I'd planned on doing. I started out sweeping the floor and filing, gasping for air when the likes of Jack Radcliffe or Joe Thomas would stop by. I soon became a man-about-the-office, learning a scary amount of the scary world of dirty publishing. And there's been not a chicken in sight.

But it's time to clear my head and 'fess up. I've been two-timing you guys all along. I have another job, too. It's the reason I wound up in San Francisco in the first place.

I work for an airline, as a stewardess. That's right: "seat-belts, please."

Some of you will be really turned off by that. Comes pretty damn close to show tunes, doesn't it?

There's emotional trauma associated with being a bearded stewardess-pornographer.

I kept myself a pariah to both worlds. Sure I'll go fetch another beer for the jerk in seat 52C. But behind my smile and professional demeanor I work with naked men and dirty pictures, so don't think I'm going to take you too seriously. You can't touch me.

Sure I'll love doing work on a magazine, but behind my eagerness I work for an airline and I'll be heading to Tokyo from here at mach .8 in a few hours. You can't touch me.

Well, I got what I wanted.

No one touched me.

Of course I had sex, that's not the point. The point is that soon I *had* to spend my weekends in far-off places and my weekdays pushing smut, or else, well, I wasn't anyone then, was I? No one would like me. Meanwhile, pieces of me started rattling off like from an old pickup on a bumpy road. For half a decade I was dragging my sorry ass off a 747 after 12 hour flights, only to drag that self-same sorry ass to the office to prove to God and everyone I could stay on top of things. Sometimes, I really did stay on top of things. Sometimes not.

So one morning I woke up, called both jobs, and said I'd be away for a while.

It was an explosive decompression. I had five years' worth of phone calls to return, and friends to spend time with. I joined a gym, rented every video on the planet; I saw that the sun still rose in the morning and noticed that my phone still rang.

Publishing is in my blood now. It's what makes me happy. But in order to move ahead, sometimes you have to be willing to move back. I went for the big union wages and weekends in Sydney. And for *BEAR* I do a little consulting, a little writing, field a butthole or two for possible publishing fame.

Downsized the jobs, kept the big dick.

Below is what I really look like. The picture you may have seen here in issues past is a fella that works for *BEAR*. You can sure as shit write to him here at the shop—and even see him get naked and make a hell of a lot of noise in that new video they're selling hereabouts.

Thanks for letting me be totally self-indulgent. This almost sounds like a giant personal ad here. But to tell you the truth, for once, I just wanted to be me.

Luke

Is That All There Is?

RTO [Reno-Tahoe Outlands] has asked me to explore the "Defense of Marriage Initiative" that Nevada's voters approved in November 2000, and will vote on again in November 2002 (in Nevada, if voters approve an initiative in two consecutive general elections, it becomes state law). Before you have the chance to vote on it again, I plan to investigate it thoroughly, including interviewing folks involved in that effort. But to begin with, I thought I should investigate exactly what language Nevada voters tentatively approved. (Since I didn't move to Nevada until mid-March 2001, I didn't really know the Initiative's substance.)

When I went to the library to research this month's column, I could hardly believe that the entire "Defense of Marriage" text fit on one standard page! The full text, which would become Section 21 of Article 1 of the Nevada State Constitution, reads, "Only a marriage between a male and female person shall be recognized and given effect in this state." Well, to its credit, it's not bureaucratic jargon, and it reads pretty simply on its face. But that doesn't mean I like it.

According to the Arguments for Passage included with the Initiative, its proponents freely acknowledge that it is currently unnecessary ("a Nevada statute provides that marriage may only be between a male and a female"), but voice their fear that "gay marriage" may eventually be permitted in some U.S. State

("a legal marriage that [takes] place outside Nevada is generally given effect under the 'Full Faith and Credit Clause' of the
United States Constitution. ... [I]f same gender marriages ever
become legal in another state, under the Full Faith and Credit
Clause Nevada could be required to recognize such marriages
entered into legally in another state"). Therefore, the Initiative
is merely a pre-emptive strike in case—some day—men may
marry other men, and women may marry other women,
anywhere in the U.S.

Why are they so afraid?

- Do they fear the ruin of civilization as they know it?
  Probably. But none of the countries that has permitted
  various forms of gay unions has gone to hell in a hand-
  basket: Holland, Denmark, Sweden, Finland, *et al.*
  seem to be going about their business as usual. Even
  Vermont, which in 1999 passed the most sweeping
  domestic partnership legislation in U.S. history, still
  seems intact on the map. (Ben & Jerry's is still running,
  and that's all that matters to me there.)

- Do the Initiative's proponents fear that their marriages
  would somehow be "cheapened" if gay people can
  get them, too? Maybe. Given the state of heterosexual
  marriage, and even many heterosexuals' hesitance
  to enter into that institution, perhaps they should be
  afraid. If our relationships can withstand lack of societal approval, and can thrive without societal reasons to
  stay together ("for the sake of the children" or "because
  I'm economically dependent on him"), nothing keeps
  us together but love and determination.

- Or do the Initiative's proponents really fear parity
  under the law for all people? When gay people request

equal rights to those granted heterosexuals, somehow this translates into some straights' brains as requesting special rights. However, I think we would wait in vain for them to admit this.

On the other side, in the Arguments Against Passage, the Initiative's opponents argue that its passage would subject gays and lesbians to different (discriminatory) treatment under the State Constitution. They also argue that the Initiative runs contrary to Nevada's public policy supporting equality and civil rights for all Nevadans. (Additionally, they point out the Initiative's redundancy, since marriage in Nevada is already an institution restricted to one man and one woman.)

Why are *we* so afraid? Even if the Initiative passes, we won't lose anything we currently possess. But some state may eventually pass "gay marriage," and that's where that Full Faith and Credit Clause comes into play. For example, if Vermont went one step further and granted gay couples marriages which conferred all rights (state and Federal) granted to heterosexual couples, Kurt and I could visit Vermont for a weekend, get "married," bring our certificate back to Nevada, and expect the state to honor our relationship like that of any other couple married outside the state. (Personally, I would prefer Hawaii—the weather is much nicer, and I could work on my tan.) If that option became available, many lesbian and gay couples in Nevada would likely want to take advantage of having their relationship recognized under the law, whether or not Nevada voters or its Legislature ever institute such a law.

And while the Initiative noted the financial impact of Question 2 as "None that can be determined," that appears misleading, whether intentionally or not. If voters pass the Initiative, then it will likely fall to the Nevada Supreme Court (and perhaps the U.S. Supreme Court on appeal) to test its constitutionality. Since it appears discriminatory on its face, no impartial judge could reasonably conclude that it supports Nevada's public policy supporting equality and civil rights for all Nevadans. (A similar lawsuit was struck down in 1998 in Colorado by the U.S. Supreme Court after years of struggle.) But I don't know enough about Nevada politics yet to predict how our Supreme Court judges would react. However, guess who will pay for the fight? You, the taxpayer! Doesn't it seem like a waste of your taxpayer dollars, whether you are gay or straight?

Since we'll be exploring this topic for a while, let me leave you with two issues to ponder:

1. Remember Darva Conger? Does the name Rick Rockwell ring a bell? A couple of years ago, the Fox network aired a television show entitled "Who Wants to Marry a Multi-Millionaire?". Fifty women entered a two-hour beauty contest-like affair on national television to see if the mysterious man would choose her for his bride. At the end of the evening, Rick chose Darva, and they were married. (Unfortunately, the unconsummated "marriage" tanked when Darva came to her senses; she quickly obtained an annulment.) But at the moment of their ill-fated marriage, they possessed more rights under the law than Kurt and I did after more than ten (now twelve) years together. But that's the way the law works. Does this seem fair to you?

2. The Initiative "provides that marriage may only be between a male and a female." There appear to be two categories the Initiative's supporters fail to recognize: The intersexed, and transsexuals.

- Some people have ambiguous genitalia and/or the genitalia of both sexes. How would the Initiative's supporters choose to classify them? (Chromosomal tests could prove that a "female-appearing" person might not demonstrate an XX ("female") chromosomal structure, even if "she" did not know it. And a "male-appearing" person might not demonstrate XY ("male"). Several other options abound, including XXY and XO. So who would the State decide these people get to marry? Anyone?)

- And what of a male-to-female (or female-to-male) transsexual? For purposes of the Initiative, are they male, or female? If they are classified by the gender of their birth, then a male can marry a female (even though she was born male), and vice versa. If they are classified by the gender they now claim as their own, then a female can marry a male (who was born a female), and vice versa. It's very interesting that the Initiative's supporters operate under a dualism that acknowledges only "male" and "female" persons. However, that's a 1950s notion at best. There are many more "gray areas" in the realm of human sexuality than they recognize. I sense the Initiative's proponents really prefer to support marriages by people occupying "proper gender roles," rather than marriages between non-gender-conforming "male" and "female" persons.

Enough for now. If that's all the Initiative is, my GLBTQ friends, let's keep on dancing. But come the first Tuesday in November, we'll have to eschew the dancing for the voting. In the meantime, please register to vote if you haven't already done so. This fight matters.

Paul

Self Diagnostics

You know what your problem is? Cuzz you have one. You've got a major malfunction, staring you right in the face, dude. Seriously.

Aw, but don't take it personally. It's because you're a human, that's all. Humans are cuckoo.

As I grow old and introspective, I am finding that everyone has some major cock-up in their brains, preventing them from getting what they really want. It's what makes us what we are. And has a lot to do with why we're still fighting wars, and why I still don't have a flying car. Even if you confidently pooh-pooh psychology in all its forms, you can't argue that people are kinda nuts. We do the opposite of what we say, say the opposite of what we mean, and the closer we get to something we really want, the more likely we are to screw it up.

Yet we have to make sense of what the people around us are doing. Humans are all we have; I have no intention of marrying outside my species. Cows make lousy co-workers—and even worse drivers. Thus, we must cut through the crap of others, and more importantly, pay attention to what kind of signals WE are throwing out.

Chances are, you make damned little sense to the others in your life.

Each of us has a *desperate* need out there, whether to be taken seriously, to be universally loved, to be famous, to be

A-List, to be clever and cool ... and we'll never attain it because we're human, and humans are fuckups. Our programming won't allow it.

We can adjust our behavior to be a little more success-ful, though.

Ponder the scenarios below; you'll see what I mean. And you won't take it personally, for even if you know me in real life, don't go thinking I'm writing about you behind your back. These examples can be found in any group of humans.

You probably know the guy who craves attention so much that he simply *has* to be the center of activity. He'll try so hard that people find him annoying and back off, making him start his dance all over again.

Or a man who's perhaps wonderful in all respects, but lonely enough that when he does get your ear, he'll talk it bloody. You steer clear of him, which banishes him to his loneliness, where he will recharge his batteries and vocal cords for the next chance to TALK.

I dare you to deny that the biggest complaint with the Gayniverse is that "everybody is a FLAKE OUT THERE!" You hear it again and again. We all want good friends and close connections. That's fine. But what actually seems to be going on is this: He who cries "flake" is so persistently demanding and pestering that people have no choice but to slither away and not return his phone calls.

For we all want love. We'll be goddamned, though, if we'll let ourselves get stuck to the heel of some other queen's boot.

I had a boss who *needed* everyone to trust him. Wull, except he was a fuckin' little liar, and everyone knew it. So why didn't he just quit lying? Or easier still, why didn't he just accept that he was a fucking little liar and stop needing everyone to trust him? All I know for sure is that he kept up with his lying ways, and was subsequently promoted to regional president.

We've got the "I must control you in order to serve my own wicked ends" guy; we've got the "I must have sex with everyone out there so that they will love me" guy (and thank god for him, right?); no social group would be complete without the shy sensitive guy who believes in true love and romantic dating—only he's sucking everyone's dick behind the recycle bins.

Since I'm lashing out with such mean and horrible examples of human behavior, it's only fair that I tell you what my "thing" is. In addition to needing to be the center of attention, along the way I decided I must be taken seriously—nay, *adored*—by the A-Bear crowd. I wish to be loved and honored by the uber hotties, and to keep one for myself. I can say this out loud because—trust me—they know. The A-Bear crowd's had my number for ages. For the most part, they've been fairly gracious about it, but I've never actually been invited to marry one. Doubt I ever will now.

To that end, just last night I said something dumb on the internet to someone I was desperately trying to impress. He's gone. Over it. And thus with the words and clever playfulness of which I'm so proud, I've shot myself out of the saddle once again.

Circuit complete.

An interesting side note to all this is that you can't tell someone else what their problem is. Try it, I dare you: They can't hear it. The information they most need will simply bounce off their skulls, their eyes will glaze over, and they'll drool and dream of ice cream like Homer Simpson.

So. Here we are. Needing and wanting, with none of us plugged in the right way.

When you see people dancing for their needs, don't be cunty about it. You don't have to grant their wishes, but you can take a deep breath and be nice. Pop Quiz: Would gossiping about them later be appropriate? Circle one: (Yes/No)

Think about what signals *you're* throwing out. What do you want? Are you making sure you'll never get it?

The most helpful thing I've figured out is to just slow down. Back off. Don't push or be in a hurry. Just listen to the clues, enjoy the pretty people.

When you calm down, they'll calm down too.

Luke

The Dilemma

The other day, while I sat on our new blue leather sofa/recliner with our cat Mumsy (as I am now), catching my breath for ten minutes before preparing for work, the doorbell rang. As I looked out the living room window, I spied a tiny boy and what appeared to be his father. When I opened the door, the little cub scout entered into his labored spiel asking whether I would like to buy a chocolate bar to help him attend a Boy Scout jamboree (or some such event). Dad stood behind him, coaching him all the way. When the boy finished his recitation and looked up at me, I felt fiercely torn.

Now, I'm a really good queer. I support all the "right" companies like Volvo, Subaru, Ikea, and Absolut (even though we already have cars and furniture, and we don't drink vodka), and I boycott all the "wrong" companies with their antediluvian policies, like Coors, Cracker Barrel, and Carl's Jr. (although I did like the Western Bacon Cheeseburger 10-15 years ago). My husband Kurt and I support many gay (and non-gay) charities whose vision and goals appeal to us. And this year, for the first time in probably 20 years, I withheld my annual winter Salvation Army contribution. (But I didn't enlighten any bell-ringers, either.)

The Boy Scouts' anti-gay policies infuriate me no less than any of the "bad" companies above. (Let's not even talk about the U.S. military.) And my husband Kurt was an Eagle

Scout, for heaven's sake! But policies become abstract in the presence of a seven-year-old. As our rainbow windsock flew gaily on our front porch, reproaching me every moment (shouldn't Daddy have clued in?), I scrounged up $2 for a Nestle's Crunch bar and a sheet of coupons, including pizza discounts and a free admission to Reno's Big Top Scout Show in April. (Of course, my waistline needed neither the chocolate nor the pizza. But I digress.)

Now I want your opinion: Did I do the right thing?

I honestly don't know. My activist self certainly didn't think so. I had half a mind to explain to my unbidden visitors that BSA's anti-gay policies forbade me to make any monetary contributions to the organization, thereby enlightening the little scout's father to the breadth of homophobia and its pervasive, pernicious effects.

But the other half of my mind wouldn't let me do it before this darling, nervous little boy. In addition to all the other dichotomies by which we can divide people, I have my own: Some people think it's more important to be right than to be kind. For the most part, I would rather be kind than right.

In this instance, I chose to do the kind thing. But I still don't know if I did the right thing. What do you think? What would you have done? (Or what did you do? I don't think the Boy Scouts targeted me alone.) Would you have any internal conflict? Please write and let me know.

Paul

Riding Bareback on a Trojan Horse

It's not like anything we've known so far. The world keeps on moving. We still have running water, Star Trek is still on TV, the economy's pretty good, and we can take vacations in Palm Springs. Most of the time it doesn't feel like we're suffering the worst domestic devastation since the American Civil War. But we are. Every day we face a strange and painful death. And in too many cases, our family and straight friends look the other way.

Fun, huh? We really know how to party. No wonder we Hom-Sexshalls find solace in rich, drunken English bitches and all those pretty rainbow flag colors.

Jesus, we've got enough risk management techniques and safer sex guidelines to gag a maggot. I personally have enough free condoms in my drawer to melt into a 1970s dinette set. And they're still peddling them down on Castro Street.

It ain't working.

I used to believe we're all trying to stay alive here. We're not. About the time that I, a college graduate and ostensibly HIV negative person, did knowingly shove an HIV-positive dick up my butt without a condom, I realized how easy it was to do. How good it felt. How many excuses there can be to "try it just this once." Thing is, a year later, I was going for broke. In 1995, I had blatantly unsafe sex with nearly a dozen men here in San Francisco.

Totally dumb and deranged? I was beginning to think so. Then I learned I'm not alone. People smarter and saner than me have also been going out and getting real stupid. HIV is spreading faster again, after a few years of slowing down. So what's going on?

Well, we're over it. Some HIV-negative guys withdraw; they refuse to get involved with HIV-positive men, and practically won't leave the house without a latex barrier. Others walk the middle line, stay safe, date, and try to hold on. For them, the losses keep piling up. My theory is that people don't stay in the middle forever. Because a big chunk of HIV-negative gay men are just plain giving up. It's easier to go with the flow—and a hell of a lot more fun. It's a path of least resistance, and there's plenty of company along the way.

AIDS turned 15 this past June (it's a Gemini—no fuckin' wonder they can't track it down). Everyone knows you're supposed to put a condom on it. That should've fixed everything. But it didn't, did it? Safe sex sucks and everyone knows it—they're just too polite to say so. HIV-positive men's dicks taste just fine (my personal theory that HIV-positive men have a saltier taste has, through many informal trials, proved false) and the real, honest-to-gawd naked feel of the inside of a man's butt is too cool for words.

So, in the first place, we're human. Clinical information about something we won't see or feel for years just don't cut it when you got a hairy 220-pounder with a monstrous weenie breathing down on you. "I'm negative. So don't sweat it, lemme slide this big ole' dick into your hole and I'll fuck ya raw. It's OK."

You can talk someone into unsafe sex in 10 seconds or less.

Then there's just plain guilt for being healthy while others aren't. Easy. Makes you feel like shit.

Now here's where it gets really twisted: In a city like San Francisco where most gay men are positive, you get inundated with the HIV-positive way of life. All the benefits, systems, services, and monies are focused on people with HIV. And they damn well should be. Subsequently, if you wind up with HIV, you have to make some sort of peace and live with it. You pick up and keep going the best you can, even when it hurts. San Francisco's full of gorgeous, gym-going, vibrant HIV-positive men. You hear things like "sooner or later everyone'll have HIV and it'll be a treatable chronic condition (for a mere $3,200 a month);" "it's just one more step along the way;" "I'm not convinced that HIV even causes AIDS, I think it's a conspiracy."

This rationale that keeps some men going is the very same rationale that others can use to end it all for themselves and join the club. This is why the rates are climbing.

I once told a guy that I was putting myself at risk of HIV. He pretty much snapped back, saying, "Well, it isn't that big a deal. You'd still live a good 20 or 30 years after seroconversion." He retired two months later, "for health reasons." He was a psychiatrist. Now, you wanna tell me we don't have a problem here?

So it's no wonder that gay kids coming out today might think there's not much reason to stay alive. A death sentence was cast back in 1981. Guys born that year are driving cars already and'll be in the bars before long. It's our responsibility, whether we're negative or positive, to teach them they don't have to go down with the ship.

HIV-negative support groups have cropped up to keep gay men negative. This really pisses some people off. It sounds whiny and callous at first. But are HIV-negative men supposed to simply shut up and act normal? Show me a human that can be all strong and "okaaaay" at a time like this without turning the wrong cheek from time to time. People act out their denial, guilt, fear, and sorrow in some damn crazy ways. It's time to recognize this and to arm ourselves with more than just condoms. We're all going to need help getting through this.

If you're HIV-positive, come sit on my face. We're all with ya, fella. And since I got this pile of condoms, you and me can try on each one of 'em; I'll keep you up till breakfast comes.

But if you're HIV-negative, don't check out on us, dude. You're needed. We gotta get ready for Act Two.

Luke

Lucky Mrs. Ticklefeather

Dorothy Kunhardt, Simon and Schuster, 1951.

In May, I "went home" to Antioch, California to prepare for *Leading the Parade*'s first "on the road" reading at The Open Book in Sacramento. My brother had been digging around in "our" closet (now his again, as he recently returned to live with my mother), and found several items that triggered more-than-half-forgotten childhood memories before producing the real treasure. (I'm getting a lump in my throat even as I type this.) I'm certain it wasn't my first book—my mother taught me to read by age three. (Thanks forever, Ma.) But my tattered copy of *Lucky Mrs. Ticklefeather* could only have been so careworn because I literally read the covers off of it (I was not a destructive child). As tears came to my eyes, I sat to read it again, and its magic still captivated me.

A simple, 32-page children's book, with nice, unadorned illustrations, *Lucky Mrs. Ticklefeather* was a Little Golden Book (remember those?). My mother purchased it for me for a quarter, and I figuratively devoured it. (The remains adhere with 35-year-old Scotch tape.) As we begin, our heroine, thin, old Mrs. Ticklefeather (curiously, no Mr. Ticklefeather appears—her bed is clearly a single; perhaps she is a widow, but certainly no gay divorcee), lives on the top floor of a penthouse with her anthropomorphic pet puffin, Paul (that must have delighted me—my name in a book! Little did I know!).

Life is swell, but she tells Paul that she wishes she had a sunflower for her beautiful big vase. (Perhaps money is tight in the Ticklefeather household; otherwise, why not just buy one?) The next morning, she awakens to find Paul missing, and she begins to cry for her lost pet. (Why does that illustration still elicit tears in me? I actually tried to crayon her tears away – very unlike me. I must have wanted to assuage the pain of losing something one loves, and the resulting loneliness. As a child, I deviated far from the typical 1960s "boy script," with my tender heart and love of kindness and beauty—is that where the "queerness" started?)

But our heroine springs into action, ringing the police. (Today I sense she would perform the search herself, but I guess "damsel in distress necessitates external hero" was an unavoidable Fifties convention.) A policeman immediately appears at her doorstep (fanciful in 1951; inconceivable today), and Mrs. Ticklefeather tells him her woeful tale. While diligently searching for Paul, the policeman finds several incongruously juxtaposed items (a pillow on a train cowcatcher, a frog on a schoolteacher's shoulder) before discovering a wheelbarrow containing a puffin feather. Questioned, the wheelbarrow's owner guiltily acknowledges selling the puffin to Mr. Macaroni for his birthday dinner. The policeman reaches Mr. Macaroni's home just as he sadly raises his axe to kill Paul, who holds a beautiful sunflower in his beak. (That picture, too, brings tears—and reminds me of O. Henry's *Gift of the Magi* and the pathos of the lovers' unselfish sacrifices.) The policeman stops Mr. Macaroni mid-swing, and purchases an enormous fish to substitute for Paul. Mr. Macaroni accepts the fish, and releases the reprieved puffin. Paul flies home to Mrs. Ticklefeather, the policeman solves his case, and our heroine reunites with her beloved pet (and displays the desired sunflower). *Exeunt.*

Of course, *Lucky Mrs. Ticklefeather* isn't important litera-
ture—certainly not to you, gentle readers. But I hope you can
find (or even recall) your first relevant book, and remember
how it influenced your life. Clearly its theme resonated
within me in a way my pristine science fiction Little Golden
Books didn't (I'm still drawn to people-overcome-relational-
obstacles-type entertainment that resolves happily). And
my "baby" brother (how *dare* he be 29!) sagely observed that
just examining our bedroom that evening provided obvious
clues as to our futures: My myriad childhood books presaged
my love of reading (and writing); every computer toy imag-
inable evinced his interest as a computer game tester and
programmer. And our wise, loving mother encouraged us to
be our unique selves, and permitted us the freedom to do so.
I hope you were as fortunate as we are.

Paul

Another Day in Paradise

Hey, dude, nice to see ya! You want a beer? Lemme getcha a beer. Here ya go. Sitchyer ass down here and tell me how it's going these days.

Damn, it's a sorry night here, ain't it? We're talking Ugh-Lee. This bar is totally hit or miss, and tonight it's definitely a Miss Thing, know what I mean?

Still, I let that one over there—you see him, by the pinball machine? Yeah, the skinny one, I let him eat out my dirty ass last week behind the bar. Whaddya mean, "Ew!"? He's got a fucking hot tongue. He likes doing it, too. He can do mine, I guess, as long as I don't have to see or smell his. Well—it's true.

Man, I had the best weekend. See, my buddy Jimbo and I went over to the Stone Lair and started drinking beer and smoking cigars, then lit up a few joints out on the back patio. This guy started pissing—up into the air. The motherfucker could shoot his hot piss clear across the patio, man, I'm not kidding. Then you know that one guy, works at the TV station? He pissed on me too, right by the beer bottles all stacked up. You won't believe this, but when I went to the can there was this hot motherfucker, beard down to his tits, made me suck his big, fat, juicy dick. You know the guy, drives a Harley and lives in the Heights and works for that telecommunications thing? Yeah. And I see his house once 'cause I went there for a foursome, and he's got like all these antiques and …. Anyway, he shot his wad and we laughed, and I was feeling pretty good.

So we went over to M–'s house and put on some porn and I watched him fuck that bartender over there, and, Jesus, it was messy. So I left. I'm not into that. So we're wandering down the street and stop by this bar and they're fisting some guy on the pool table. Turns out they already had the cue ball up there, and we all were drinking Jagermeister shots and smoking some 420. I don't think I got home until 4:30. Still. I was feeling pretty good.

Woof! Who's he?

You know D–? He tried to have a lover. I know, right? You know who with, though? T–! Shit you not. D– and T–, trying to be all stable and shit. But it so happens that the drugged out guy with KS, whatshisname, got T– in the men's room at the Stone Lair and fucked him up the ass and came and the condom broke, so I guess him and D– aren't going together anymore. Yeah.

When I got off work yesterday, I sucked this Hispanic guy's dick at the shower at my gym. Get this: He spoke no English and had a fat, uncut dick. He just grunted and tried to fuck me right then and there, no condom or anything. Just started ramming it right into my hole. But I stopped him. Like I'm gonna let some strange Ecuadorian slobber cum up my ass? He tried following me until I got dressed and he saw my SF Police Department T-shirt that this trick left at my house, and I guess he got scared cuz he disappeared pretty quick.

You know that guy over there? Wearing the fire department T-shirt? No, not the guy wearing the New York Fire Department T-shirt, the one right next to him wearing the Santa Monica Fire Department T-shirt. Yeah. Know him? You do? Doesn't he have the nicest dick? God. I love his dick.

What's the matter?

You OK? Hmm?

Wait. Don't tell me. You and HIMMM? REALLY? Breakfast and flowers? Jeez. I never woulda thunk that, him trying to be stable and romantic, especially after I saw him all strung out on crystal meth at the dungeon last night fucking some twink without a condom. Shit, he musta pounded that kid's ass for an hour.

What? What's the matter with you?

You can't seriously be liking on him, can you?

Take my advice. Never fuck someone you're attracted to. It just doesn't work. I've been in this city for 22 years and only the faces and dicks change. And really only the faces change, you only got about 18 styles of dick to worry about and after that you've pretty much seen 'em all.

You got a nice dick too, you know, you need to get out there and use it more. Everybody's looking for dick. I don't care if they say they're a top, the minute they catch sight of a decent cock those legs just go right up in the air. Like that one over there? Doesn't he look like a mean motherfucker? Well. I've seen him take fists and feet and—get this—he likes to eat out of a dog dish while wearing a leash. So you just really never know.

I know what your problem is. You're all wanting to fall in love and get something special. I see you do it over and over and over again. As soon as you meet a guy and find out he isn't a virgin and pure, and the minute you find out that someone did him the week before—BAM. That's it. You dump him cold.

Well, nobody wants to see you hanging around like a puppy in love.

The only way to survive in this town is to keep your head down and fuck. It's like—the minute guys fall in love they disappear. They move away and start driving Jeep Grand Cherokees and doing potluck dinners on the Peninsula. They're never heard from again. Until someone dies or they break up. They're right back here next to you and me, practically lapping the piss out of the urinals.

This is our natural state, buddy boy. Get over it. Just go with the flow.

It feels pretty good.

Luke

The Fan

On my first mini-book tour this spring, I've had some fun and interesting adventures. But the best one came at A Different Light [bookstore] in Los Angeles. It was my second day in L.A. reading to small but enthusiastic crowds. After completing the reading, while I was speaking with friends and signing books, my *favorite* writer walked into the store. I couldn't believe it! There was Joel Perry! Now, if you aren't familiar with the gay press in southern California, you may not recognize Joel's name or his work. He's written a humor column for *Frontiers* for quite some time, as well as for national gay magazines *The Advocate* and *Instinct.* Joel's humor and mine mesh together so well that his writing has been known to make me orgasmic. (I've screamed "Yes!" several times while reading his work, sort of like Meg Ryan in *When Harry Met Sally.*) He also wrote a great book of essays, *Funny That Way: Adventures in Fabulousness*, that I adore. No other writer has made me laugh out loud so hard and so consistently. And here he was, walking into the bookstore at the end of my reading! Thank God it wasn't during it; I'd have been so tongue-tied as to become incoherent!

In his presence, I became both uncharacteristically rude and bold. I quickly excused myself from the friend with whom I was speaking (sorry, Shane!), ran up to Joel, and breathlessly blurted out, "You won't know me from Adam, but I know you're Joel Perry and I am metaphorically falling at your feet right now." Perry looked as startled as the proverbial deer caught in the headlights. (An appropriate metaphor, as my husband Kurt says Joel has "doe eyes.") I then explained how I had been reading his *Frontiers* column and loved his book. Noticing his still stunned expression I exclaimed, "This must happen to you all the time." Joel replied that not only had this *never* happened to him, he had never even been recognized by the cover photo on his book before. As it turned out, he came into A Different Light because he recognized a mutual friend who attended my reading and just dropped in to tell Steve "Hello." We talked for a minute or so, during which he told me how thrilled and humbled he felt by my recognizing him, and we left with a wonderful bear hug. (Also appropriate, since we are both "bears.")

Since then, we've written each other a couple of times. In one of his e-mails, he insightfully pointed out, "We all know there's no money to be made in gay publishing. We do it for the love and to minister to our Tribe. But money isn't everything. I've found that the real riches lie in the wonderful and amazing people you get to meet through your work." He's right, you know. I don't expect I'll ever get monetarily out of my book what I put into it in time, etc. But as a writer, it's special when someone connects with your work. And while money would be nice, we really do what we do for love, and it's fantastic when someone else completes the circle with us. So please don't ever think that the influential people at the forefront of our movement aren't approachable; my entire book, as well as my encounter with Joel, should refute that theory. And if you find that my work touches you, please feel free to let me know. I give really good hugs, too!

Paul

Absolutely Positively

Things've been going really cool. Bought a motorcycle and have learned to go vroom, which I now do as often as I can. Vroom. You should try it. The pulse quickens. And I've been working out, getting beefy—for the first time I've started to feel all right with what I see in the mirror. To complete the urban-gay-male-in-his-30s picture, I've also been pricing real estate in San Francisco to maybe buy a piece of this tectonically challenged rock.

Yup. Things've been going really cool. So when the counselor lady came back to me at her desk with a piece of paper and said, "Your test results came back positive," I felt like somebody took all the air out of the room.

Last week I became just another San Francisco fag with HIV.

It's OK; my insurance company already knows, so we can talk about it. And I'm not going to whine. Promise.

I really thought I had the risk-management thing licked, though. Evidently not; I seem to have licked entirely the wrong paradigm.

Maybe you read a column from before about how it's been hard to stay HIV-negative where most people are positive. I guess I let down my guard. But the absolute fucking pissant part of it is, I was getting back on track, engaging in far less risky behaviors this past year. I was scheduled to begin HIV vaccine trials. I thought I was going to get through this.

I'd been tested every six months as part of a study group. All my sexual activity was dutifully noted with the Centers for Disease Control in Atlanta; I could just imagine some underpaid southern belle with really long fingernails entering my deepest kink into an old Ray-O-Vac mainframe going, "Lilly-Mae, look at this one over hee-ya!" My blood would be drawn, and I'd come back ten days later. My counselor lady would go get the slip of paper and come back and say your test came back negative. Well, she didn't say negative this time. One little word came out wrong, and this is going to be really bad for my complexion.

I've never been so mad in my whole fucking goddamn life. For the first time ever, I wanted to beat the living shit out of somebody—anybody. I couldn't eat for two days. Feeding myself felt like feeding "it" inside me, feeding those nasty unseen little buggers in my bloodstream. Well, that part didn't last too long. I soon threw myself headlong into a cheeseburger and bowl of tiramisu. Now I pretty much feel OK, but manage to quietly freak once or twice a day for no apparent reason.

An HIV-negative friend asked me if it's a relief to finally seroconvert.

Nope. It sucks.

Someone else said that once you convert you don't have to worry about safe sex anymore: You can just go out and fuck and fuck as long as the other guy's also positive. It's the '70s all over again.

Nope. Now they've got protease inhibitor-resistant strains that no drug can fix. Not to mention some nasty African blends that'll take you out in six months.

Did I somehow believe these things? Did I do this on purpose? I honestly don't know. I can't even pinpoint the actual moment of infraction, although I have a few suspicions. All of them tasty and sweet.

Trying to digest news of this magnitude is going to take some time. Yesterday I came across an estate sale on Castro Street, right up above the pharmacy. You see, people die here, and we get to buy all their stuff. An apartment filled with pictures, books, CDs, and clothes, all priced to move. This was the quintessential gay man's apartment, full of the smell of cigarettes and all the stuff that mattered to him. With the life gone, it was just so much junk. So of course I'm picturing my apartment after I'm dead, the things being sold, my family wearing black veils and fighting over my furniture.

I just had to go be a fag in San Francisco, didn't I? Now look what happened.

Some of you have already been through this and are muttering, "Get off the cross, Mary; someone needs the wood."

Well, I need to go through what I need to go through.

There's hope nowadays. It's not a total death sentence, although it promises to be a downright pain in the ass. And it could kill me. That's some heavy shit.

If you think too hard about living, dying, the futility of the universe—hell, it would be impossible to get out of bed in the morning. I know. I've tried it. (You're looking at a fella who once got depressed thinking the human race will eventually die out, only to be replaced with cockroaches, and how cockroaches would look real shitty in leather and how awful it would be to eat lunch in a cockroach restaurant.) Yet if you don't happen think about anything at all, then you're just as liable to step off a curb and get hit by a truck. So here again, it's one of those balance things. Maybe it's all right to play dumb when I get sniffly and scared. I don't have to worry about the inner workings of my lymphatic system every minute.

Our basic instinct is to remain alive. Shit, in a city like this you can see people who honestly want to die fast. I know a guy who takes as many loads of cum up his butt as he can get, which, given his good looks and accessible Castro location, equals five or six wads a night. Honest. But the human body is a resilient little fucker. He wakes up every morning and makes a pretty nice day out of it.

We're alive until we're dead. Realizing we're not going to live forever has got to be one of those important life-lesson things you hear about. And someday I'll come to that realization, too. Until then, though, I refuse to constantly look over my shoulder.

I think the Grim Reaper should lick my infected asshole.

Now go and enjoy the naked men here in the magazine. I'm gonna go ride my motorcycle.

Luke

One Nation Under God?

I pledge allegiance
To the flag
Of the United States of America
And to the republic for which it stands
One nation
~~Under God~~
Indivisible
With liberty and justice for all

When I was asked to write for my church newsletter, I don't know if this is what was expected. (In fact, I'm pretty certain this is not at all what was expected!) But this issue has touched my heart, and I appreciate the opportunity to share my views.

On June 26, 2002, in a 2-1 decision, a panel of the Ninth Circuit Court of Appeals (representing most of the Western states) issued a ruling that the phrase "one nation under God" in the Pledge of Allegiance (or, as my atheist friend Doug calls it, the "Prayer of Allegiance") that children recite in America's public schools "amounts to a government endorsement of religion in violation of the separation of church and state. Leading schoolchildren in a pledge that says the United States is 'one nation under God' is as objectionable as making them say 'we are a nation "under Jesus," a nation "under Vishnu," a nation "under Zeus," or a nation "under no god," because none of the professions can be neutral with respect to religion," Circuit Judge Alfred T. Goodwin wrote. ... However, the ruling will not take effect for several months, to allow further appeals. The government can ask the court to reconsider or take its case to the U.S. Supreme Court." (*San Francisco Chronicle*, June 27.) Most Christians and politicians (including the entire Senate) have decried the Court's ruling, but I believe the Court has done the right thing.

One of this country's founding principles was separation of church and state. Our founding fathers wanted to avoid the situation they saw in England, where the government officially endorsed the Church of England (which itself split from the Catholic church when Henry VIII wanted a divorce it would not sanction), and in effect denied its citizens and residents equal access to non-government-sanctioned religions. As a result, my denomination, the Universal Fellowship of Metropolitan Community Churches (UFMCC), has had great difficulty over the years attracting English adherents; despite evidence that most of England's great church edifices host pitifully few worshipers, state sanction makes those who do attend church far more likely to attend C of E services, rather than some non-sanctioned upstart church.

And why was "under God" ever added to the Pledge of Allegiance in the first place? Again, the *Chronicle* reports, "Congress inserted 'under God' at the height of the Cold War [in 1954] after a campaign by the Knights of Columbus, religious leaders and others who wanted to distinguish the United States from what they regarded as godless communism." Only a year earlier, President Dwight D. Eisenhower signed Executive Order 10450, which gave the federal government authority to discriminate against homosexuals in its hiring practices. Both of these actions were designed to assure and protect the majority of "good Americans" from "bad people"—Commies and Queers. Only these people weren't necessary "bad"— just different. Do we really want 1950s' ideals of conformity (and intolerance of diversity) to rule our nation in the third millennium? I surely do not.

Many gay people regularly encourage the heterosexual majority to take into account and be sensitive to the different needs of the GLBTQ minority. From my vantage point, I think it should always be the moral responsibility of the majority who control a nation's societal power (in our society, white male Christian heterosexuals of means) to ensure protection of the beliefs and rights of its minorities (non-white, non-male, non-Christian, non-heterosexual, and financially impoverished people). I realize this is not the way our world works today, but it should be our highest aspiration. (As Jesus said in The Sermon on the Mount (Matt. 5:46, 48, NIV), "If you love those who love you [or are "like" you], what reward will you get? Are not even the tax collectors [i.e., the world] doing that? … Be perfect, therefore, as your heavenly [Parent] is perfect.")

Today, even a non-Christian American would likely tell you that the United States is primarily viewed, and operates *de facto*, as a Christian country. As Christians in a primarily Christian society, we must learn to be sensitive to others' religious beliefs (or absence of beliefs), which we must assume are as important to them as ours are to us. Far too often, Christians unthinkingly assume that while God loves us, God doesn't love those whose beliefs differ from ours.

Along those lines, should Christians force their religious beliefs upon non-Christians (a practice generally known as proselytizing)? Here I confess I once did just that; upon knowing "the truth," I was led to believe that I was responsible to bring that truth to a dark world in need of Christ's light. In teams from my church, we knocked on doors, and shared with those who would listen. (And I did not grow up a member of the Church of Jesus Christ of Latter-Day Saints (Mormon) or a Jehovah's Witness, two denominations well known for proselytizing.) Today, it would be unthinkable for me to take such an action.

Would I dissuade someone from becoming a Christian? Absolutely not! But would I attempt to "force" Christianity upon someone else because I knew it would be good for her/him? No. Here's a parallel example: Would I "out" a closeted gay men or a lesbian because I knew it would be good for him/her? Again, my answer would be no. Someone else's religious beliefs are to be chosen between him/her and God. If asked my opinion, I feel a responsibility to share what I know and believe. If I see someone struggling in life with no spiritual beliefs whatsoever, I can offer what works for me. But if someone is comfortable in his/her faith (or absence thereof), then I have no business barging in to tell that person that Christianity is the only way to connect with his/her spiritual higher power. Given my upbringing, that may very well be true for me. But my spiritual truth is not everyone's spiritual truth. (There's a lesson for Christians in that, too.) And I don't think God has a problem with that, either. God wants those who love God and seek to worship God to be free to do so. God never forces us to love God. And woe unto us who feel we must step in where God does not tread, forcing people to acknowledge a God they do not know (and perhaps do not care to know).

When I recite the Pledge of Allegiance (should that situation ever occur again), in my heart (if not with my lips), I'm sure I will always say "under God." But I don't want a seven-year-old Hindu-American child (or an atheist) to be forced to say it. Not in the America I love. The land of the free and the home of the brave. With liberty and justice for all.

Paul

Top It!

When gay fellas start going on about sexual tops and bottoms, I can't get a certain image out of my head. I shouldn't be telling you this, it's deeply personal. But at first I didn't know what all the top/bottom fuss meant. I just didn't know, OK? Leave me alone.

The picture that came to mind was of my two older sisters. They fought endlessly over a stuffed toy kitty cat named Kitty. I remember. He was pink and white with a big ribbon around his neck. So once—oh, this must've been when the oldest was about 8—they got into a tug-of-war and ripped the fucking kitty in half. One got the kitty tops, one got the kitty bottoms, and they kept their respective parts for years. I don't remember now who got which.

Kitty Tops and Kitty Bottoms.

So here's me, years later, standing in a bar in Washington, D.C., when some guy wearing what looks like a Nazi postal worker's uniform made of questionable leather swaggers up to me and demands to know if I'm a top or a bottom.

Miaow.

I was polite. Never wanting to dis someone going out on a limb in a social situation. I said something like, "Why, yes, I am, thank you for asking ...."

Well, he didn't like that. He muttered something and wandered back to his friend who, coincidentally, was dressed like an Argentinian parking warden (Peronist era, I'd say, 'round 1958). I think I heard a "tsk" from the second one; can't be sure over such loud disco music.

The truth is, I'm both. I'm neither. I'm ... hell, I'm confused. But I have real good sex just the same.

And the first thing out your mouth?

"Yup. Luke's a bottom."

Because, to those who worry about such things, it's a common belief that he who refuses to be labeled must be a bottom and is overcompensating.

What? You mean, like, a stereotype? Hmmm. Never ran into one of those before.

"That's a bottom's perspective." "The older a gay man gets, the more he just bottoms out." "Pushy bottom." "Sloppy-Wet-Pass-Around-Party-Bottom."

I'm sure you've never made such claims toward a fellow gay man. But some people do.

Why does it carry such a stigma, this being a bread-basket of gay sexuality? I think it's partially because it's being on the bottom is being vulnerable, and you can't be caught dead being vulnerable. Mostly, people wanna be topped. We want a big strong hairy bearded fella to call the shots so we can relax. So we can get fucked. Goes back to the daddy thing, and maybe it's all sick and dysfunctional but it sure feels nice.

There's a difference in emotional punch between the two roles. Your assignment: Get your dick sucked by someone you don't know. Cum. Then, on a different night, get on your knees and suck a strange man's dick. Smell his balls. Don't cum. I bet in 80 percent of you, the servile act was much more exciting, more heady, more dangerous to you. Even when you didn't cum.

Then there's butt-fucking. It's a heavy thing, having someone rummage around your intestines with his prick. In my experience, getting fucked is much more emotionally charged. Physically you're at your most vulnerable, and it's one of the headiest taboos we can get away with. But to tell you the truth, after about three minutes for me it loses its charm. Getting fucked up the butt is damned annoying, and I get a queasiness that lasts well into the night.

I've got a big dick. So I usually experience the joy of being a top and of pushing men over the edge. It's an ego boost, sure, but it's very sweet. It's something I can do for someone, and, when done right, can create an incredible bond. Oh, and fucking butt feels really choice. It's good.

Some major Australian leather columnist picked me up in a bar and got all tough and started giving orders. He tried, anyway. I just wasn't in that sort of mood. I started playing with his butt and ten minutes later I was fucking him hard. I then went down on him and ate out his butt and then started to put my hand up his hole, only to be replaced with my tongue or dick. He didn't know if I was going to kiss him or fist him and he was absolutely breathless. He couldn't speak. He just kept gasping and moaning and I showered him with sweat because it was a hot night in Honolulu and I really could have put my hand in there, I think.

It was wonderful, and I'll never trade the pleasure of riding herd on a man. Ever.

I'm both. I'm a top and a bottom. They come from very different places in my head. The bottom part is sultry, emotional; it's very right-brain. Sometimes I practically purr and start backing-up against the furniture with a twitch in my tail. The top part is much more flighty. It's dirty, it's aggressive. I look at the thickness of a man's thighs and torso and wonder at which angle I'm going to gore his belly from the inside with my dick. It's the sex where you don't want coffee and conversation.

One time I was really jonesing for some butt, really wanted to fuck someone, but couldn't for the life of me find anyone interested in being on the bottom. A rather sardonic fella who used to work here at *BEAR*, when I lamented to him of this, said, "All you gotta do is go out and flag bottom— whoever you bring home is bound to be a bigger bottom than you are, and you'll be all set."

And there was the time I was making fun of another *BEAR* co-worker who was a leather top and wore all the gadgets to prove it. I rigged up a tire rim, chains and a 14-pound lead weight and walked through the office dragging my collection on the floor behind me—from my left-side belt loop, to be sure. "I'm a top. Notice me, I'm a top." I almost got decked for it, but it felt good.

Jesus, if you can't have a sense of humor, whatever you are, do us all a favor and just stay home.

In the meantime, bottoms up.

Luke

Radical Harmonies

(documentary), Woman Vision, 2002. 88 minutes.

I have a confession to make: I think I'm a lesbian trapped in a gay man's body. Why else would I feel so strongly moved by lesbian lives? I love potlucks (if not tofu), and may purchase a pair of Birkenstocks any day. But seriously, folks, I've had the privilege of knowing so many fantastic lesbians, including women's music pioneers (and I plan to interview more this summer for another lesbian/gay history book) that it really feels like "my" community. While in San Francisco a few months ago to experience the premiere of "No Secret Anymore" (discussed in March's *Outlands*), I purchased a copy of this new, fascinating documentary detailing the history of "women's music" in America.

Women's music grew out of labor, civil rights, and peace movement music in the late 1960s/early 1970s. While many of its pioneers were heterosexual (witness Sweet Honey in the Rock, Kristin Lems, and Holly Near in her early days), lesbians eventually made their way to the forefront of the movement. Foremothers like Maxine Feldman ("Angry Atthis"), Alix Dobkin ("Lavender Jane Loves Women"), and the women involved with the Olivia Collective in the early 1970s (including Cris Williamson and Meg Christian), along with many less-famous women, created music that spoke to women's souls. Many relationships and loving partnerships developed (and some disintegrated) among the artists, producers, and promoters. Music that explored women's loving relationships with one another empowered and transformed lives. And the music itself has changed over the years, becoming more raw and fierce.

However, as occurs in any "movement," problems naturally arose. Should men (and later, straight women) be permitted access to concerts? What roles would women of color and working class women play in the movement? Should the music be "spiritual" or "political"? (Later, should male-to-female transsexuals (as opposed to "women-born women") be permitted to attend festivals?) But the struggles (the "process," if you prefer) ultimately empowered the women. Along the way, women developed production, promotion, engineering, and distribution networks exclusive of men's participation. Women's music concerts and festivals simultaneously developed many important cultural innovations, including sliding-scale fees, interpreters for the deaf, the valued role of volunteer festival labor, and special service provision for the differently-abled. Today, women's music taps the mainstream through performers such as Ani DiFranco, Bonnie Raitt, the Indigo Girls, and Melissa Etheridge. But this movement opened the doors for these and other talents to walk through proudly.

Radical Harmonies explores these topics in the voices of the women who fought the battles and (mostly) emerged victorious. Illuminating archival footage intersperses with their heartfelt stories. Perhaps most moving is the experience of Wanda and Brenda Henson, who brought a women's music festival to Ovett, Mississippi in the early 1990s. The Deep South was not prepared to receive the message; in fact, "good ol' boys" very nearly killed the messengers! Their transformation from timid women to Amazons exemplifies the power of women's music—Wanda describes it as "better than baptism."

OK, I guess I'm not really a lesbian. (Thank goodness! I'd hate to give up sex with men!) But maybe women's music resonates so strongly within me because of its intrinsic power. Too many gay men express disinterest in lesbian history and culture (and vice versa). As much as lesbians would learn from watching *Radical Harmonies*, men (gay and straight) would discover so much more. Broaden your horizons; branch out. We *are* family—so get to know the other side of your family tree!

Paul

There's a Cat Turd
in the Sandbox

We're coming up on my seventh anniversary in San Francisco. All these years and I'm still stuck on the same damn thing I was when I got here:

How do you find the love of your life when you're trashy?

Eighty percent of my hobbies and lifestyle are about being a gay bachelor in Sin City. I stewardess to England, Hawaii, and Australia for sex; I play on the Internet for sex; I hang out in the Castro for sex; go to potlucks, the Lone Star. All my friends are gay men. It's fun. It's liberating. There's dried sperm on my PowerBook, and I don't even know whose it is. When family comes to town and I have to put the penises away, I'm all antsy and feel, even though I really love my family, like I'm missing something or being cheated. Even if, on my own here in the Cit-Ay, I haven't actually *had* sex, or for that matter, even the threat of sex recently. It's the hope, the expectation around sex that becomes a drug.

Yet, however, hang on a sec: I've also longed for the big-all-come-to-Jesus relationship, the one with harmony, eternal lust, and baby talk at dinner parties. The man will be gorgeous, and pure as the morning dew.

What we have here is a basic conflict of interest. It's fun to play in the sandbox of sexual freedom, but I don't know how to mix that with the desire for a quiet, mature romance. You can't have both in my mind: A relationship starting out that open isn't the relationship I want. Sure, I can see having a healthy, happy open relationship, but only after a few years of monogamy and building up some trust. Somehow, I just can't do both at the same time. Not yet, anyway.

It's easy to get hurt out there. God forbid you should actually like someone. That's just asking for trouble. Listen. You'll hear what I mean:

"Oh, I had him. He's a good kisser, but he'll only let you do him once."

"Oh, hey, Luke, I fucked your cop last night. You're right, he's hot!"

"Which issue was he in?"

"There's really only twelve gay people in the world, the rest is done with disco mirrors."

"You might have better luck giving him a hardon than I did."

"He's a pig, ain't he? Had to pull his lips off my asshole so hard you could hear a smacking sound."

All these things (and more) have been said to me about men I was starting to date—some seriously.

No, there are no virgins. I'm only half kidding about the morning dew part. But this One Degree of Separation shit gets real old. When you meet a man you like, you have to start with the knowledge that he's already fucked half your friends, and at some point, they're just going to squirm with joy at telling you every detail. It sucks. It's impossible to maintain a mystique that's so easily dashed to bits.

Part of it is my own jealousy issues. I'm working on 'em. I started my sexual career by dating a man who'd slept with half the state of Colorado. Men, women, orgies, drugs, eating pussy—he'd torture me with tales of evil. We were together over three years, lived together. He got fat and ugly and I loved it that way. We had all straight friends. I'd forget about his evil past until every once in a while at a dinner party he'd have too much Merlot and start talking about his history. The orgies. The bookstores. The drugs. I'd freak. Wasn't until near the end of all this that I realized more than half of my jealousy was because I hadn't had the chance to do any of those things myself. Not the pussy and drugs, but the orgies and sex sex sex.

Back in 1990, still wet behind the ears, I went to work for a dirty magazine in San Francisco.

I've become the very person I was most afraid of.

(I've had regrets. There was the guy with really gross icky teeth, my buddies and I joked that he gave my dick gingivitis. There've been a few bunny-boilers out there, too; *Fatal Attraction* lives as a viable social skill for some.)

Fucking around *feels* harmless. That is, until you find someone you like. The stakes can go from zero to sixty in nothing flat.

No one's going to stop fucking, and they're sure as shit not going to keep quiet about it. You either have to become jaded and cynical, or just stay home and rent videos instead. And I'm not happy about either option. Nobody likes a sour bitch, and nobody even *knows* about you if you stay home. To sit around pissing and moaning about the lack of intimacy in gay culture is to commit social suicide. No one wants to hear it. If the crowd at your bar or bookstore or Elks lodge gets a whiff of emotional need from you, they'll probably get scared and drop you like a hot rock.

I try to separate what's my own personal problem and what's not. There's something vexing about the gay community, yet it's so ingrained that people just drink and fuck to avoid looking at it. Yet I'd like to learn how to turn off the jealousy and expectation I feel when I meet a new fella. That'd definitely help.

Does this happen to anyone else?

Luke

Sacramento's Lavender Library

On June 3, it was my pleasure to speak at Sacramento's Lavender Library, Archives, and Cultural Exchange about my book, *Leading the Parade*. I had done readings before, but this one was special: LLACE co-founder and director Gail Lang asked me to speak with her group about the "dish" I learned along the way, and I was happy to oblige. Even for you die-hard fans who read *Leading the Parade* (now available in the Washoe County Public Library System—thanks, Larry!), I couldn't possibly say everything I wanted about each individual I profiled. So to prepare for the presentation, I reviewed virtually every transcript of my conversations (probably about 4,000 pages or so) to refresh my memory about some stories I didn't tell in the book.

After giving the audience a quick synopsis of my interviewees, and mostly in response to their questions, I shared with them stories about Sacramento's role in GLBT history (including former San Francisco Supervisor Harry Britt's opinion of the City and writer Kate Millett's involvement in the first women's music festival there in 1973); movement founder Harry Hay's crossing out his inscription to me in my copy of his book; historian Jonathan Ned Katz's harsh response when I asked him for an interview (and my blunt reply); President Jimmy Carter's willingness to permit gays and lesbians to serve openly in the U.S. military (and national gay organizations NGLTF and HRCF's disinterest); the role of Sacramento's own "Ann Bannon" (my hostess) in literarily killing a dog because her fictional character could handle her "nervous breakdown" better than she; a special meeting between gay journalists Mark Thompson and Randy Shilts; and Rep. Barney Frank "getting laid," among others. I also shared the story of my husband Kurt walking in on my interview with East Coast lesbians Barbara Gittings and Kay Tobin Lahusen wearing a button that said, "HELP! I'm living with an unpublished writer," and how we all cracked up. That only scratched the surface—I'm going to publish a book many years from now called *All the Things I Couldn't Say*. My receptive audience of about 30 folks also became the first to which I spoke as an award-winner! (*Foreword Magazine* selected *Leading the Parade* as its 2002 Bronze Medalist for Gay/Lesbian Nonfiction, an honor I discovered only the day before.) I don't care *what* Harry Britt said; Sacramentans are fantastic, and I'm beginning to consider the place my home away from home!

Why do I tell you all this? Because history doesn't have to be boring! (Especially not the history of a sexual movement!) Gail encouraged me to present a program that would not be simply a recitation of facts, and we made it interactive and fun. June was Gay History Month (sorry I'm a little late), so why not go to a library, bookstore, or video store to read or watch some gay history (there is no shortage of wonderful documentaries, a painless way to enjoy history if ever there was one!). Better yet, go out and *make* some gay history!

Paul

Where No One Can Hear You Scream

It's time for a little readership participation. Fuck this "sitting-on-your-ass-and-letting-the-folks-at-*BEAR*-do-all-the-work" shit. You're going to be involved. In fact, you already are involved, and you just don't know it yet.

Today's topic is one that no human can avoid for very long. There is no escape. You, dear reader, have participated in the most horrific catastrophe the world has ever known:

THE DATE FROM HELL.

Of course, you weren't THE date from hell. You were ON the date from hell. Right? It's always the other guy who's weird. Right? You're perfectly normal.

Right.

The way I see it, there's several types of dates from hell, listed here alphabetically: Bunny Boilers; Call Waiters; Chemists; Porters; and WFWs (Way-Fucking-Weird-For-Absolutely-No-Discernable-Reason-Whomsoever'ses).

Bunny Boilers (*lapinus cookeroonius*) love you. They can't live without you. The classic Hollywood example is, of course, Glenn Close, who stands in the kitchen screaming "I won't be IGNORED!" and who tries to cook a rabbit to impress her married boyfriend, only she forgot to remember that murdering your intended's child's fluffy pet is usually construed, at least by our society, as being mildly eccentric. Yes, murder is always a subtle clue. Other red lights: He calls four times a day even before you first go out, and seems just a little too interested in you. If he's hanging on every word you say, it means he has nothing of his own to hang things on. Another sign? BBs preach tolerance and love, but if the waiter brings the wrong thing, watch your date's reaction. One normally doesn't go postal over cappuccino foam. Run, quickly. Change your phone number.

Call Waiters (*cellularium hangapussius*) look great. They got the beeper, the cell phone, usually a nice car, and they love to make sure you don't get an inflated sense of Self. They've always got somebody on the other line, literally and figuratively. Oh, and the Daytimers(TM)—they just love to pencil you in. They SAY they use ink, but you know better. If your date french kisses absolutely everyone you pass on the street, including women, and constantly takes phone calls, you've got a problem. "I'm sorry, I'll just be a second .... Go ahead? Oh really? What did he say? They're going to break up, aren't they? ... Sorry, I'll just be a second." Face it. You ARE the second, and you always will be. A Call Waiter should only be kept on hand if he has a humongous dick and knows how to use it.

Chemists (*snortus fumeroleum*) are usually soft and amiable. All your ideas and opinions will be met with a "Yeah, totally!" Any disagreement or strife will be met with a "huh?" Bodybuilders are usually in this category too—hormones, don'tcha know. These people love to sleep, so they're particularly good for the winter months. Their bedroom will have a slightly moldy smell; their refrigerator will be bereft of any food-type things. They're always late or don't show up at all, but when cornered, they get all affable and sweet. Chemists will do almost anything you say, you just have to watch for the flipside: "I'm Satan now! Watch me BURN!"

Porters (*Loveyus Howellus*) are loud and flamboyant. The stars of every scene. Never going anywhere without Baggage; they bring steamer trunks full of agony. The past boyfriend who lied and cheated! His car that got stolen! Porters usually have had several wildly divergent careers, such as airline executive, Pentecostal minister, and porn star. He probably got shipwrecked in Jakarta, and his father never understood him—all this information (and more) spills forth on the first date. Fascinating stories, flaccid dicks.

WFW (not translatable) is essentially an umbrella category for the purposes of analogy. Makes for much easier target practice. Way-Fucking-Weird-For-Absolutely-No-Discernable-Reason-Whomsoever'ses can run the gamut of the above-mentioned characteristics, but these guys add spice to any date. Some personal examples I've encountered? Well, let's see. There was the guy in Haight-Ashbury who, while I was riding his rump, kept plopping off my dick and running into the next room to snort poppers, only to return and start fucking again. Did this several times, like I was going to steal his poppers. A friend of mine also wound up having the exact same experience with this guy.

I like threeways, and they create an exponential growth in dating weirdness. I went on a date with a couple, one of whom somehow didn't manage to tell his partner that we were supposed to have sex. It disintegrated into quite an argument in their front hall—with the first one trying to French me while his lover was yelling at us. I've also gotten pawned off onto one of the two men as some kind of consolation prize. That's good for the esteem.

Let's see; one guy hit and abused his cat on our first—and ironically only—date; one guy vowed up and down he wasn't in a relationship but would only have sex with me in his car (and parked on these San Francisco hills, you can really see the face of God); a married one who was the hottest man I've ever tasted but who gave me his home phone number only to have his wife answer the phone. Such learning experiences on the road of life. How can we be so lucky?

Just don't get me started on the guy who tried to suck my dick in a freight elevator, that's a whole 'nother column in and of itself.

Where do *you* come in with all this? You're gonna write down some of your own personal dates from hell and send 'em to me. The Luke File, *BEAR* Magazine, 2215R Market St. #148, San Francisco CA 94114. My editor Rich won't mind having them pile up on his desk—I've seen that desk, and trust me, you won't even make a dent. The winner of the most horrible awful date from hell—substantiated and verified—will receive a date with ME!

Luke

That Was the Week
That Was

[While reading this article, feel free to play "Celebration" by Kool and the Gang]

Guess what, gang? We've "won" the culture war! Better yet, "they" know it! If any doubt remains, witness the progress made during one week (OK, ten days!) in June, when Canadian Prime Minister Jean Chrétien chose not to appeal an Ontario Court of Appeals' decision to Canada's Supreme Court (thereby legally recognizing same-sex marriage in Canada), and the U.S. Supreme Court struck down sodomy laws in the thirteen remaining states that carried them. These are hardly our first legal victories—Deb Price and Joyce Murdoch's excellent book, *Courting Justice*, demonstrates several noteworthy successes. The American Psychiatric and Psychological Associations decided we were no longer "sick" in the mid-1970s, and most mainstream churches continue to struggle with our degree of sinfulness. But for our Supreme Court to overrule its decision a mere 17 years after *Bowers v. Hardwick* (in which the Court found that Georgian Michael Hardwick had no right to engage in consensual sex with another man) in deciding that the State of Texas unfairly restricted John Geddes Lawrence and Tyron Garner's right to engage in consensual sex is nothing short of extraordinary. (In historic contrast, it took nearly a century for the Supreme Court's 1857 *Dred Scott v. Sanford* and 1896 *Plessy v. Ferguson* decisions to be overturned by *Brown v. Board of Education* in 1954, belatedly affirming African-Americans' rights to participate as full citizens in American society.)

The Court's 6–3 decision, penned by centrist Judge Anthony Kennedy (who writes in pertinent part, "*Bowers* was not correct when it was decided, and it is not correct today. ... The Texas statute furthers no legitimate state interest which can justify its intrusion into the personal and private life of the individual"), and concurred separately by fellow centrist Sandra Day O'Connor (who sided with the anti-gay majority in *Bowers*) proves we now occupy the middle ground in America, further marginalizing our opponents.

(Tellingly, in dissent, Justice Antonin Scalia writes, "Today's opinion is the product of a Court ... that has largely signed on to the so-called homosexual agenda .... It is clear from this that the Court has taken sides in the culture war .... Many Americans do not want persons who openly engage in homosexual conduct [participating in their daily lives]. They view this as protecting themselves and their families from a lifestyle that they believe to be immoral and destructive." Scalia then disingenuously adds, "Let me be clear that I have nothing against homosexuals ...." What's next, Tony—"Some of my best friends are gay"? *Tres cliché.*

(Curiously, even dissenting conservative Justice Clarence Thomas adds, "If I were a member of the Texas Legislature, I would vote to repeal [the statute]. Punishing someone for expressing his sexual preference through noncommercial consensual conduct with another adult does not appear to be a worthy way to expend valuable law enforcement resources.")

In recent years, the "battle lines" were drawn fairly clearly: Roughly one-third of American adults consisted of openly gay folks and our supportive family and friends; roughly one-third disliked us so strongly, for whatever reason, that we had no prayer of reaching them. Our struggle has been to sway the middle: Those with no vested interest in gays achieving their civil rights who were not predisposed to hate us. All of our visible efforts as a community over the last 30 years or so—from local gay pride parades and festivals to the Marches on Washington; from television to movie representations depicting our vast diversity; from our martyrs to our saints; from our response to AIDS to our creation of local and national organizations—have contributed to painting an accurate portrait of our community. As Holly Near sang, "We are a gentle, angry people." We are also a funny, silly, serious, political, stylish, loving, in-your-face, *fabulous* people—and mainstream, heterosexual, Middle America knows that now.

But the conservatives' white flag of legal surrender conceals weapons of queer destruction. While celebrating victory, we must anticipate a backlash, as right-wingers witness one of their most precious prejudices de-fanged before them. As "they" have already begun constructing a Constitutional amendment to exclude recognition of gay marriages, we must remain (or become) active. Winning the culture war will not prove sufficient alone to gain us our full civil rights, including legal rights in relationship recognitions in every state, adoption, immigration, military service, domestic partner benefits, etc. Let us also recognize that our victory does not protect all members of our LGBT community (specifically, the "T"), and remain vigilant on their behalf as well.

With newly-conferred rights come newly-developing responsibilities. While not all of us will be "model citizens"— nor do we all aspire to be—we must acknowledge our responsibilities and take them (if not ourselves) seriously. This does not mean that we should necessarily ape heterosexual culture; its models are not always (or only) appropriate for our community. But if northern North America now seems prepared to offer us equal civil rights, we must not squander them frivolously—for example, a "trick" is not a marriage, nor is raising a child a "trendy" fashion statement. Gay people must prepare to confront issues such as alimony and child visitation rights—when the law excluded us, and in the absence of accepted precedent, we could (and often did) walk away from our relationships, leaving destitute partners (or being so left). Americans preparing to trek northward to solemnize their marriages also must understand that any subsequent divorce will require a one-year residency requirement; two people should not undertake such a decision after a wild weekend simply because they now can.

How will the next GLB(T) generation develop, knowing that their most personal sexual acts are no longer criminal in nature, and finding increased recognition and sanction of their relationships? This is the fruit of the labor of so many—to create a better life for those who follow us. I hope it will more closely resemble the raspberry than the grapefruit.

Paul

Zippity Doo Dah

Being gay is better than being straight.

Sure, we got our problems, not the least of which was having to be a fag in junior high school. For most of us, gym class was like having Auschwitz for fourth period.

But being a grownup and being a fag is a blast. Usually. It's important to remember that.

In a lot of ways, gay men and women have a little bit more on the ball than straight people—simply because we had to grow up with a secret. At some point, you and I had to look in the mirror and realize we're gonna come out a lot different, and there's no escaping it. We're a minority, but our parents aren't. That's some heavy shit for a five-year-old. Until a few years back, homosexuality had such a bad PR problem that it just kills me when straight people assume it's a choice on our part. No one would have picked this. It chose us, and we can just go off and fuck if we want. But I digress ....

We have an edge. We've had to look harder and step much more carefully. It builds character.

We can be both: Straight or gay, as we please or need to. Well, some of us have just a little too much taste and flair to confuse the world for long. But done right, it can be a hell of a lot of fun; like the T-shirt, "Don't feed or tease the straight people." My sister's still not over a comment I made a few years back. She lives in a rural small town, and when two bubbas drove by in a big 4x4 pickup with a gun rack, I said, "You don't understand. In San Francisco men drive trucks like that BECAUSE they're gay."

Yeah, we can play it straight when we need to, and then laugh all the way to the bank.

Straight men have a lot of work to do. They have to follow sports. That alone is almost enough to put me off pussy. It's such hype, and there's so much pressure behind it. If a straight man doesn't like sports, there's something seriously wrong with him—a library scientist trapped in the body of a heterosexual. Have you ever been on an airplane only to have a quiet flight interrupted by six men in six different areas of the plane who start to go "WHOOP! <clap-clap-clap> YEAH!" from under their headsets? It's the Game, you see, they just heard a good touchdown thingy.

I can't think of any other occasion where people yelp and hoot loudly in public. But straight men have to. They know that, as soon as the plane lands, their client will grill them on the latest game, and they'd better know the answer or it could mean losing that new account.

Sometimes, though, I feel sorry for straight men. For one thing, they've got to date women, and having sex on a female human's terms is problematic at best.

Now I LOVE women. They're the coolest. I think gay men have a better understanding of straight women and that pisses straight men off no end. Ha ha.

But a stewardess friend of mine is a girl; she's gorgeous, and single, and trying to date. I'm sorry—the things I hear her going through are so far removed from the problems I have as an urban gay man. She hasn't had sex since February. I haven't had sex since yesterday. She must go on two or three dates before sex will (or is allowed to) be brought up; she tells me the goofy, immature things men say to her, trying to get into her panties while trying to seem like they care.

God, what a mess. You've probably noticed: Straight culture is a lot more geared toward finding a mate and keeping him/ her for life. It's the whole family values thing. I wish them luck.

Now for me, just last week, I fell into a raunchy three-way sex pig session with two complete strangers on a moment's notice. I HAD been on the way to the bank, but a better deposit opportunity came up, so I took it. That's the way it is when you're gay in San Francisco. Wish I could remember that one guy's name, though—he had a nice butt ....

Straight men face death by stoning if they admit to masturbating. Was sitting around with a bunch of clever waiters with taste, and we were discussing how often we beat off. One turned to the only heterosexual guy in the group and said, "How often do you jerk off?" The man screamed: "I don't! If I need sex, I find a woman!" And he ran out of the room. No lie. He later apologized, and was so blown away that we could sit and have such a conversation. I think he was impressed.

As with all things, the key is to just be. When you know who you are and what you want, the rest doesn't matter. But there's a danger: it becomes real easy to sit back and make fun of other people and the way they are.

Ain't it great?

Now I'm not trying to pick a fight. Straight/gay, top/ bottom, bear/not-bear—hell, I hate people who install the toilet paper roll so that the paper hangs down the back—I think they're stupid. We're not all alike, and we should celebrate our differences.

That's all, I guess. Just remember these things when you take your Crixivan, when you have only a cat to call family, when you piss and moan about the lack of intimacy and the return of platform shoes. We got it pretty good. I quote a waiter I used to work with. Before he died he often sang this song to that old Disney tune: "Zippity-doo-dah, zippity-aye, my, oh my, it's great to be gay; Suckin' him slowly/suckin' him fast. Or turn 'im over and bugger his ass."

Luke

National Coming Out Day

In honor of the 15th anniversary of the first National Coming Out Day (October 11), I revisited my interview with NCOD co-founder Jean O'Leary in October 1994 to review our remarks about the events that led to its inception, and some of the controversy that surrounded it. I have edited our remarks for clarity.

J: [Leadership in the gay community is] one of the most thankless things you can possibly do. Sometimes I wonder why anybody does it. … I know for myself, I was really clear about what I was creating. And that's the only thing that kept me going. … I knew the changes I was making. You know, I was trailblazing! And it was very, very hard on me.

P: You were conscious of it, then.

J: I was totally conscious of it. And that's why, when I look at the movement, and people over the years, you know, are depressed in one way or the other, I have *never* been depressed about—I've been very affected, especially by AIDS. But with the exception of that, every trial that we've had, I just see it as a stepping stone to eliminating the greater prejudice. Which has been our invisibility!

P: Right.

J: And I have never lost sight of that. And that's why, being co-founder of National Coming Out Day, why I took on that project, it caused so many problems. It was so unpopular the first year. You would have thought I was resurrecting Hitler, or something. "Why do we need this? Why are you bringing people out of the closet? Why are you forcing people out of the closet? This is too slick." You know. Coming up with all these cups and newspapers and hats to promote "National Coming Out Day." I got so criticized for that. And within my own organization [as Executive Director of National Gay Rights Advocates], it caused me tons and tons of trouble.

P: So it really started out rocky from the get-go? NCOD?

J: Oh, yes! Very! Yeah, in fact, the first year was the rockiest. And then from there, it was—you know, it became institutionalized. And now it's probably our most popular national holiday, and I think it'll just grow and grow and grow. ... It's amazing what you can start, if you have appeal and a vision. And you know where to tap in, because that's where we're going, and what's gonna last. And it's just amazing, how many people try to tear it down while you're doing it. Until it becomes untouchable. Or institutionalized.

P: How did [NCOD] really get off the ground?

J: OK. I don't know if [Rob Eichberg, the other co-founder of NCOD, and I] have exactly the same recollections of this. But it was at the War Conference, in [February 1988], that there was—this was one of four issues. … The concept came way back from the "We Are Everywhere" concept. And that if everybody turned lavender tomorrow. I mean, that's obviously—it's the root of our movement. And no one can take credit for this idea. But it was there on the table at the War Conference. … It was being brought up here, as—well, you know, "Is anybody gonna do anything about this?" And I said—

P: Do you remember who presented the idea?

J: No, I don't. Rob says, I think, that he presented it, at the conference. … When that idea was presented, you know, I said, "I want to do this." And I went to Rob, and I asked him if he would help me do it. And then I said, you know, "Can we both go up to the microphone and present this?" And for two reasons I wanted to do that. One, because Rob would be a beautiful counterpart to me, and I knew we would make a wonderful team. Me being so political, and him being so personal. And secondly, because I knew that if I just stepped out and did this without consulting my Board of Directors, and so on, I was gonna be in big trouble. And I wanted to have the back-up, just in case. But here's a case of seizing the moment. I didn't have time to go back and ask my Board of Directors all this. It was a very important thing that wasn't gonna get done. I *knew* I could do it. I was committed and passionate about it. … It was me! And it was Rob, too. … It had always been coming out, coming out, coming out. Every speech I made. Everything. This is the essence of our oppression, is our invisibility. Etc., etc. … And so I went over there, and I said, "OK, Rob. Let's go." And so we both went up to the microphone. And said, "OK. We've volunteered to do it. National Gay Rights Advocates and Rob Eichberg of The Experience." So then, I took the operation back to NGRA. And brought it in under the auspices of the organization. ... I hired two people to be full-time people, working on National Coming Out Day. And that's when I think the shit started to hit the fan, you know.

P: Over at NGRA?

J: Yeah. It was, "Where are the resources going here? Are we a legal organization, or are we a political organization?" I.e., Jean O'Leary and [1988 Democratic Presidential nominee Michael] Dukakis, and everything I was doing with that. "Or are we some kind of grass-roots thingy over here doing National Coming Out Day?"

[Ultimately, and amid controversy, O'Leary stepped down from NGRA, which closed its doors shortly thereafter.]

Feel free to use National Coming Out Day to take your next step out of the closet and into the sunshine! (Or, if you're like me, and you have no steps left to take, encourage someone else to do so!)

Paul

Spit in the Ocean

This one's been weird to write. Whatever this column does to your head, it's already been toned-down for general consumption.

You probably already know, if you've read my pedantic whinings in the past, I became HIV-positive in late 1996. Shock, dismay, hope, drama—the usual. I was never going to have sex again. Two months later, when I nudged the head of my naked dick into an HIV-positive friend's butthole, when the only thing between me and eternity was a thin coat of spit, I thought I was going to explode. I suddenly remembered what all the fuss was about.

You know what? A lot of us diseased critters've been bareback fucking each other's brains out for months now.

"Oh, look, I better lick up this here spilt cum; it could stain the furniture."

"Tell ya what, you take your dick out of his butt and put it in MY butt before putting it back in his butt. We'll wash you off later. Maybe."

"My teeth are flossed, let's go suck some dick!"

And recently, the doctors have been strangely silent.

Because of the miracles of modern-day printing, you're reading this three months into my future. For me, now, it's the first week of July 1998, and the Geneva AIDS Conference has just wrapped up. "Super-HIV" was the name they came up with for this week's keen new threat. Impervious to all known drugs. New and improved. Get 30,000 extra RNA viral copies FREE with each new load of "Super-HIV"! And while they're at it, they're still fussing with numbers about whether or not you can fuck up someone's drug response by introducing your own drug responses into their viral load-thingy. We all suspected, I'm pretty sure, that it'll all be found dangerous and deadly and we all must stop. That we must put the condoms back on, before things get worse.

I recently infected an HIV-positive friend with Hepatitis B. I forgot, you see, that I'm a carrier. I've been hidden behind latex for so long the subject simply hadn't come up in over a decade. We've had bigger fish to fry. Then, this same week, a friend of mine found out he was infected with HIV. The big guns. He was out playing like he shouldn't have been. He knew I was HIV-positive, and I wasn't the only one who put him in danger—but was it me? I didn't say "no" to him. And now he's got it.

See? It's like a second wave. People are tired of waiting, tired of being good. I know a lot of HIV-negative men who say they don't care. "There's pills nowadays ...." they say.

Well, I shit my pants in line at the grocery store a while back. Some pills. They make you sick, and that's just if you're lucky.

Here's a really twisted story: I just got an e-mail from my big-dicked Canadian friend, who's HIV-negative and who came to San Francisco while I was on a stewardessing trip to Taiwan. Mr. Canada is partly the reason I have HIV. We decided, about four years ago, to have unsafe sex, knowing we were both negative. He has a husband, a doctor, who's also HIV-negative, but we weighed the risks, and wanted to give it a try. For me, it had been five years since I'd had the real thing. We fucked each other blind.

It's like the old Nancy Reagan model of, if you smoke dope, you'll become a heroin addict in six months flat. I just had myself a little unsafe poke and it cracked open a real dangerous door for me. Through the ensuing years I got more and more risky, seeking more and more thrills until one day I had the crud, and there's no going back. Did I let myself get HIV so I could have unsafe sex like I've always wanted?

Sometimes, I honestly think so.

So here's Mr. Canada, coming to San Francisco for the first time since I got cooties, and he's saying that he wants to fuck me without a rubber. Beautiful dick; my favorite. But I'm deciding that I won't even meet him. I don't trust myself. I went to the other side of the planet to remove myself from temptation. And there he went, an HIV-negative man, spitting on that gorgeous huge dick of his and shoving it up some other strange man's ass without a condom anyway.

Now I'm hurt and I'm mad ... because it wasn't me and it wasn't my ass he stuck it in.

Pretty twisted shit, huh?

If you experiment with raw, unprotected sex, you won't be able to stop. You'll get HIV. And you'll get it FROM someone, and that someone may just be trying to care for once.

There's four kinds of gay men out there: HIV-negative ones who are secure enough to stay out of trouble. I salute you. You probably think the rest of us are pathetic losers. But have you never slipped into the role of the second type of guy—the HIV-negative man who screws up occasionally? And who secretly digs it, despite the fear?

On the HIV-positive side, there are the men who do all they can to stay healthy, to minimize that yellow waxy viral buildup. Safe sex all the time. Yet how often do they lapse into our fourth category: Guys who just want to have fun, who take everything from Herpes to Feline Leukemia up their butt and still come back for more?

We all have these characters inside of us. No one wants to die all the time, any more than we want to live forever, hermetically sealed.

We've all got our choices. The choice in front of me is whether to stay as pure, healthy and bored as I can, or to damn the torpedoes and hope science keeps up with the *schmutz* in my blood.

I've spent the past week telling myself if I have to have safe sex, I'd rather have no sex at all. I'm sure I'll get over it, but seeing these thoughts come out of my head is deeply humiliating.

I'd like to add a special thanks to the queen who fucked a monkey in Africa some twenty-two years ago and started this whole thing. Missy, you're really workin' a lot of nerves.

Luke

Turning Point

Twenty-five years ago this month, the second most infamous hate crime in gay American history occurred. (Matthew Shepard's murder would probably rank first.) On November 27, 1978, former San Francisco Supervisor Dan White assassinated Mayor George Moscone and fellow Supervisor Harvey Milk.

The killings punctuated a dizzying month in the Bay Area, where I lived. On that first Tuesday, San Franciscans joined other Californians to defy the political odds and defeat Proposition Five (which, among other things, would have led to the firing of openly-gay public schoolteachers). From that short-lived high, barely a week later, Rev. Jim Jones and some nine hundred of his followers, mostly from the Bay Area, committed ritual mass suicide in Jonestown, Guyana after killing Bay Area Congressman Leo Ryan and his entourage. Two weeks later, Milk and Moscone lay dead. As San Francisco TV anchor Dennis Richmond commented on that month's unprecedented events, "To outsiders, and even to some San Franciscans, it must appear the City has gone a little insane."

Why did White's assassinations matter so much? So two politicians died; big deal. But it was a big deal to me. While living in the Bay Area in the Seventies gave me the advantage of knowing I wasn't the only gay person in the world, the three options I identified as a gay teen were A) drag queen (which terrified me); B) "Castro clone"/leather person (for which nature failed to equip me); or C) Harvey Milk. Harvey's political acumen mattered less to me than his living his life as a visible, proud gay man; I don't think I knew it was possible before then. In 1978, even as a 17-year-old carefully tiptoeing his way out of the closet, I knew I couldn't live an unfulfilling life of half-truths and shadows.

I didn't dare participate in the candlelight vigil the evening of his death; however, watching it on television, nothing had ever moved me so deeply. In the documentary *The Times of Harvey Milk*, San Francisco State University professor and Harvey's friend Sally Gearhart described that vigil as "one of the most eloquent expressions of a community's response to violence that I have ever seen. ... I think we sent a message to the nation that night about what our immediate response was. Not violence, but a certain respect for Harvey, and a deep regret and feeling of tragedy about it." (The violence came later, in May 1979, when Dan White received an eight-year prison sentence for committing two murders, and served only 5-1/2 years. (In contrast, Sara Jane Moore received a life sentence for merely attempting to kill President Gerald Ford.) Less than two years after his release, a confused, broken White committed suicide.)

A few days after Harvey died, I skipped school—for the only time in my life—to view Milk's and Moscone's caskets, listen to political speeches, and yearn for my freedom. The only way I knew to avenge Harvey's death was to do what he had always implored us all to do—come out. I began to do so with a vengeance. Ironically, within a week, my life took yet another turn that delayed my journey for almost six years, but ultimately the truth set me free.

I didn't know then that Harvey's personal life was in shambles, from his finances to his codependent love relationships.

In 1995, Cleve Jones told me, "With Harvey, I was always holding my breath, because he was always saying things I thought were stupid. ... He could be very flip. ... He also had a violent temper, sometimes. ... He had several lovers, which raises—there's also a side to Harvey that people don't want to talk about." But Harvey Milk frequently encouraged young people all around the country (like me) who clung desperately to the hope for a better tomorrow for lesbians and gays, and articulated it in a way that proved an oasis in our desert of trepidation. I'm grateful that as I approach Harvey's age—it shocks me to realize I'm only six years younger than he was when he died—my life is on much more solid footing than was his. I live a whole, fulfilling, integrated life that in my adolescence I didn't dare dream possible, and for that I am profoundly grateful.

When Harvey Milk came out of his closet, he "had nobody to look up towards." More than three decades later, when I came out, at least I had Harvey. Now, no young gay person in America can grow up thinking s/he is "the only one." And I don't think the death of any one gay person could resonate today in quite the same way it did when Harvey left us. We live in a much different world 25 years later, in this era of Vermont and Canada, of overturned sodomy laws, of *Will & Grace* and *Queer as Folk* and *Queer Eye* and *Boy Meets Boy*.

This Thanksgiving, I hope you are doing your part in your world to eradicate homophobia and to make the world a better place. If you are, please accept my sincere thanks. If not, it's not too late. Someone has to give them hope, whether they are 17 or 70. Why you? Why *not* you?

*To learn more about Harvey Milk, read **The Mayor of Castro Street** (Randy Shilts, New York: St. Martin's, 1982) and/or watch*

The Times of Harvey Milk *(Rob Epstein and Richard Schmiechen, producers, Black Sand Productions, 1984).*

Paul

Baggage Carousel Number Four

Picture the most beautiful man in the world. Picture him in your mind, or open that JPEG you like so much. Maybe the most beautiful man in the world is someone you've seen on TV or in the movies; or here in this magazine. Maybe you see him every time you look in the mirror (and if so, do we have your e-mail address?).

The most beautiful man in the world.

Don't you love that feeling?

The sight or whiff of a damned sexy man goes right through you and into your belly and balls. Beautiful men are so soothing to look at. There's a palpable difference when one walks into a room. When all else fails, a decent visual can remind you that all is right in the world.

But then you try to touch it—try to hold that beauty—and suddenly the world is a horrible place indeed.

What gives?

Technically speaking, beauty is a morphological predisposition towards physical symmetry and a low incidence of recursive mutations or weak genetic immunities. Honest. Baby kittens and pandas and even baby humans are cute for a reason: So that the adults will be eager to protect, rather than eat, the young'uns.

Paradoxically, some cute baby humans grow up to be cute adult humans, making us WANT to eat those. Nature's a very sick puppy.

Beauty was built in to create competition, selectively breed strong DNA and to keep the makers of Arrid Extra Dry in business for centuries to come. Our whole culture is based on getting things that either are, or that make us seem to be, beautiful.

We all know what it's like to meet a man who makes your palms sweat. You go from bored to breathless, from glib to goober. Must Have! Never mind if he has a lover, you can break 'em apart and get the spoils for yourself.

This is shallow, immature stuff. I'm talking about appearances and externals and things that don't last. We're supposed to be deeper than that.

But I'm not over it yet. I want me some. I'm tired of always being "the funny one."

Take *BEAR* Supermodel Jack Radcliffe. Please. He shops at my grocery store sometimes. I'll be standing there with my toilet paper and Pine Sol and bananas and there he goes—buying something beautiful, I'm sure. He totally lights up the frozen food section while I'm just the mousy guy with ten items or less. I asked Mr. Radcliffe one time what's it like being handsome to such an extent. He demurred and claimed he wasn't. Which made him even cuter, but it didn't answer my question any.

I still want to know what it's like to light a place up like that, or better yet, to be able to keep a perfect gorgeous man underfoot for a while. In all probability, I'd turn into a high-strung mess, constantly afraid he'd get bored with me and someone else would steal him.

"Gorgeous people are really screwed up," they say.

Well you know what? Ugly people are really screwed up too, only nobody gives a shit.

"It's what's on the *inside* that counts."

Well, have you SEEN what's in there? Yuck. Totally needs to be refrigerated after opening .... Besides, if you're going to put your mouth on something or get into fights over who has to scrub the shower curtain, it might as well be with someone who has a lovely exterior.

"Beauty doesn't last forever." Yeah, I know. History's full of people who married themselves up with a bo-hunk, and when all was said and done, the only thing they had left was a crude, farting imbecile who was no longer remotely appealing. But I still want to get myself a piece before I really am over the hill and ugly. The clock is ticking, gentlemen ....

Perhaps you've noticed: Beauty comes with serious baggage. Granted, it's lovely baggage ... the best. But not all of it is their baggage. Some of it is our baggage, us normal people hoping to hitch a ride and get a piece of the action.

Beautiful people, therefore, have some pretty interesting defense mechanisms. There's the ones who flirt madly with everyone, but never put out. Then there's the ones who wouldn't dream of speaking to the likes of you. They're usually mistaken for being stuck up, when maybe they're just tired of being seen as a means to an end.

There IS a lot of snottiness out there, as we all know. I do it sometimes—this thing where someone tries to talk to me but he's maybe not my type so I squirm and basically cut him dead. I'm trying to not do that anymore. Gay men love to talk only to those men they plan to fuck. I'm all fer fuggin', but when you get down to it, even the most gorgeous men actually fuck only a fraction of the people they meet. So relax. Be kind and sociable. I'm sure it doesn't mean you're going to have to marry the guy and get to know his mother.

I'm only just now starting to learn the ways in which beauty is a commodity. Beauty is quite the weapon. It's exchanged for goods and services, it controls, conquers, and perverts. Beautiful people are given automatic status. It's like being rich. You're gorgeous, you walk in, the place is yours. It just feels like if you've got good looks, you can have everything.

Here's a fun one: Gorgeous Man over whom I've always drooled, right? Turns out a friend of mine knows him. Nice guy, but he wanted this friend of mine to do him a favor. Basically, a "do my homework for me and you can fuck me, OK?" Friend said "Um ... no? Get over yourself?" Mr. Gorgeous Man was really taken aback by that. "But everyone wants to have sex with me. I'll let you do it too ...."

And suddenly, I'd finished finding him beautiful. I was at peace.

So what gives?

Beauty gives. It gives up and runs away at the first sign of trouble.

Maybe beauty was just given to us to drive us crazy and make us try harder out there. Maybe we were never meant to keep it.

Which is good. Otherwise, we classically handsome sons of bitches wouldn't stand a chance.

Luke

Lambda
Literary Conference

Attending your first writer's conference tells you that you're really a writer. I originally planned to spend a week's vacation in October hitting tennis balls in Las Vegas with the gay "seniors" (35 and up), but since I'm working on another book, I conducted three interviews instead (in Boston, Washington, D.C., and New York City) before attending Lambda Literary Conference V in Provincetown, Massachusetts.

First, you have to get to Provincetown, no mean feat from almost anywhere in the United States. I originally planned to take a ferry from Boston, but the main ferry service inexplicably canceled several of its departures. Instead of renting a car and driving three/four hours around Cape Cod (Provincetown perches at its tip), I flew from Boston to Provincetown on Cape Air (the TV show "Wings" drew upon this airline). It's not cheap, but it's quick (25 minutes) and extremely convenient. I had been in Provincetown once before (to interview Urvashi Vaid for my first book), but since I literally spent about four hours there before flying back to Boston, I really had no chance to absorb the place then.

Bring your unlimited American Express card; P-Town is expensive! They have a short tourist season (probably May through October), and everything arrives there via some expensive, inconvenient route. My small but pleasant room at Romeo's Holiday cost me $88/night, the best bargain I found in town. My burrito at Lorraine's one evening was the cheapest item on the menu—at $16.95! My nice lasagna dinner at Bayside Betsy's cost a bit less, and I found an inexpensive Chinese restaurant serving General Tso's chicken for $9.95 (less than my salad one afternoon!). Merchants sold clothing at bargain basement prices (touristy shops close there for the winter), but I didn't want to lug anything else back to Reno. And the shows! I saw the ninety-minute "Funny Gay Males" show for $18 at the Crown & Anchor. The next day singer-songwriter Cris Williamson (whom I interviewed in Seattle a month earlier) performed for an hour at the Post Office Cabaret. Fortunately, Cris comped my $20 ticket (it's good to be a journalist), but with a two-drink cover charge for soda, juice, or water, my $8 produced two half-liter bottles of water; that's about 25 cents an ounce, for you non-math majors. Bring an extra arm and leg; you'll need them!

All right, it's expensive. But it's gorgeous. Look up "quaint" in the dictionary, and you'll find P-Town. The city stretches about three miles long, and basically just two blocks wide (between Commercial and Bradford). Beautiful flowers; tidy, colorful houses and shops; ocean views for days. Since parking is impossible, one walks everywhere. Luckily, I stayed for the beginning of Women's Week, so I experienced a wonderful mixture of lesbians, gay men, trans folks, and supportive, friendly straights (with and without children). Everyone appeared relaxed and happy. Even San Francisco isn't this free and peaceful for GLBT folks. If I looked up "utopian" in my dictionary, I'd find P-Town there as well!

Where was I? Oh, yes, the conference! Following Friday's Opening Reception, we went pretty much non-stop. Each participant could mix and match course offerings according to his/her own interests. While the conference skewed toward fiction writers, I still found several thought-provoking offerings to interest me. Accordingly, on Saturday I attended a wonderfully interactive "non-panel" on book promotion (co-hosted by my publicist, Michele Karlsberg, whom I met for the first time in person after well over a year of e-mail correspondence); a panel on screenwriting (I've got a great idea for a screenplay, and I wanted to learn something about the process); a journalism panel; and then, my panel: The Art of Non-Fiction. Our moderator, Robert Schanke, asked each panelist to assemble a five-minute presentation on a particular topic—I chose how to conduct an interview and how to develop your contacts. Since I couldn't cover that much material in five minutes, I drafted handouts, and extrapolated on seven interviewing principles that novices might miss. The other panelists included Martha Stone, an editor at the *Gay & Lesbian Review*; William J. Mann, author of several good gay non-fiction works about early Hollywood and its stars; and icon Edmund White. To my pleasant surprise, White was a sweetheart: very modest and unassuming, and passionate about his work and presentation. We followed our presentations with a lively, interactive discussion, and I believe ours was the best of the panels I observed. (Other people said as much to us, so I'm not just prejudiced.)

Sunday found us all a bit more relaxed (or maybe just tired!): I began with The Fate of Gay and Lesbian Bookstores ("challenging" in our Amazon.com world), then attended The Rise and Fall (?) of the Coming-Out Novel (including participant Christopher Bram, writer of the book that became the movie *Gods and Monsters*—also a sweetheart), Getting Your First Book Published (moderated by my publicist, and including panelist Lesléa Newman, with 40 books to her credit, including *Heather Has Two Mommies*—sharp, very Jewish, and *very* funny!), and the Closing Reception. Well-known writers Alex Sanchez, Samuel Delany, and Andrew Holleran also attended the conference, but I missed their panels. I also met some young and not-so-young writers—some published, some still trying—on the cusp of fame and fortune (we hope!). I enjoyed the generosity of spirit among the writers; seldom do we know if anyone hears us, nor do we regularly receive immediate feedback. The conference proved a great opportunity to perform that task for others, and to have it reflected back to us.

Next year's Lambda Literary Conference is scheduled for Palm Springs, California (another of my favorite places). If you're a West Coast writer (or even just want to meet some great gay writers), I can't think of a better opportunity to meet some of the nicest book people around. For more information, contact the Lambda Literary Foundation at <u>www. lambdalit.org</u>. See you there!

Paul

What We Can Learn from Straight People

You might get scared: first Bush gets in the White House, and then Luke comes along and starts to preach the merits of straight people.

Jesus, what the hell's going on?

Well, don't panic there, Kyle. I haven't undergone some sort of conversion process. In case you become frightened during the discussion, or if the smoke gets too thick in here, your exits are two in the front, two in the rear with four pull-in window hatches located over the wings. Step out leg first and follow the arrows ....

Queer people are great, like I'm always saying. And I'm dedicated to my position as a cock-sucking-butt-fucking-Victorian-furniture-loving-pinko-liberal-fay-gott. You should be too. Even if you like IKEA, I still love and support you.

Straight people, on the other hand, are stupid and boring.

And have they not given us just a whole rash of shit over the years? Damn! The hangings, the beatings, the marriage thing, well ... damn.

But now we've almost got straight people right where we want 'em. They watch Will & Grace and laugh at our jokes. Homosexuality can come up in conversation and not result in stabbings. That's progress!

Our breeding stock is getting docile and compliant, like good cattle should.

So the sea is calm enough, I think, that we can discuss heterosexuality in a mature way. We're all adults here, aren't we? Actually, breeders are almost becoming a disadvantaged group these days. After all these years, now they need our help, and we are in a position to lift them out of their pathetic existence. We'll continue to teach them what we know. They'll probably get laid more, and everyone will be a lot more relaxed.

But there's a lot we can learn from straight people.

(Now you're getting scared! Floor lighting will automatically illuminate to guide you to an exit.)

First off, from straight people we can learn to laugh. Obviously. Look at their uptight manner of walking and dancing. Not to mention their dating rituals.

We can learn to be a little more patient. Straight people have always had a certain stick-to-it-iveness. Except lately as, in the last few decades, they've tried to act more like gay people and bed-hop. The idea that they're supposed to form families and to STAY that way has started to slip from their consciousness just as it's started to enter ours. Funny, huh? But these things come to mind as I enter my middle age and as the adoption of two cats forms the most responsible bond I've yet had. And as I realize I can't really ask a gay neighbor to go with me to IKEA because I would then appear too clingy.

We can learn to be sexually frustrated. True art comes from hidden emotions and from shame. Breeders sure have that in the bag. A teasing eroticism that DOESN'T end in a carpet-staining orgy can actually be satisfying. In its own way.

Gay people look fabulous and sometimes straight people don't. Maybe we should relax and get dumpy? Works for them. If I see one more gorgeous bubba driving a pickup with a non-gorgeous, amply-buttocked, unkempt wife next to him on the seat .... Makes me want to eat potato chips and watch Jerry Springer and not wash my hair. Obviously it's what straight men want in their females, right?

We can learn sports and monster truck smashing. Yes, we can! I know you're at a loss to understand WHY we'd want to, but the option is there.

We can learn to drive an SUV while plugging a pacifier back into the screaming mouth of a baby.

We can learn the duality that comes from trying to be a groovy grown-up while still having to keep our little ones from being afraid of the dark.

We can learn what it's like to have someone start to grow up in our own image, only to watch them veer off onto some path of their own and we can do nothing to stop it.

We can learn the power of heritage: Sounds like a china pattern for a really swanky party with movie stars and fabulous drugs, doesn't it? But did you know that heritage actually means generations and generations of people forming a family and serving a sense of continuity?

See? Already their lessons have faded into obsolescence, despite being the basis for life on Earth.

Being home for the holidays with family this last season really taught me a thing or two. I watched the 18 people of my current family, ranging from 74 years to four months. A feast was et. And tho I myself did not carve the roast beast, I thought about how human families used to all live in one place together, grandparents and toddlers and married straight people, fighting and laughing and lining up for the bathroom. It was warm. The food was good; I laughed harder than I've laughed in years. I learned several key Pokémon and bounced a couple of nieces on my knee so one of 'em could pull my beard and shriek. Felt like heritage. Kids really aren't all that scary, once you get to know them.

Of course, doing some speed and getting fisted is all well and good. But it doesn't further us as a people. It doesn't further anything but the Crisco and paper towel industries. It doesn't make the world a better place.

If you're smart, you're already figuring out that one of the main differences between straight people and gay people is that straight people have kids. It's a major, life-altering condition that gay men never experience—dogs not quite withstanding. If we man-loving men started having children that didn't just get flushed down the municipal equalizer, then our own culture and heritage would start to change damned quick. The music would get quieter, the bedtimes earlier. Our morning-after discussions would gravitate toward gurgles and wobbling first steps. To our nerves of steel in handling grown-up manly butt wiping we would add deft forays into vomit, snot, and rashes. And you could kiss your oriental carpets goodbye.

It would make us a little more patient as a people, I think.

So. Do I think you should go out and have kids?

Probably not. Way too many humans are being born with nowhere to go. And I don't want you to miss out on those Tuesday night nipple chews from the back bartender.

I just want to remind you that while we're out fucking ourselves silly, there's other people who are staying home with the kids. From them we can learn a thing or two.

What you do with this is entirely up to you. You can take all of it or none of it.

I just don't want you to be afraid of the dark.

Luke

Political Grab-Bag

Boy, did my editor pick a tailor-made topic for me this month! Considering that "LGBT Political Life in America" has consumed my life for the past three months, I do have some opinions on the subject! Here's a grab-bag of miscellaneous thoughts:

In January, Stonewall Democrats of Northern Nevada (SDNN) elected me its President. We have quite a job ahead of us during this Presidential election year, and I've been working to build on our good efforts last year, when we solidified our presence here in Washoe County. If you're a Democrat (or want to become one) and would like to join us, we are actively working to swell our membership roster! Feel free to contact me at outthere@outlandsmagazine.com, and I'll be happy to send you the details.

Since I began toiling in the local political fields about a year ago, I've had the privilege to work with representatives of the other local Democratic constituencies (including the Men's Club, the Women's Club, and the Young Democrats). At no time have I ever been made to feel "less than"; every Democrat with whom I've worked has been completely supportive of me personally, as well as of SDNN and our community. I'm not worried about being given a "place at the table"—it's there for the taking! Anyone willing to volunteer is enthusiastically welcomed. The Democrats are the "big tent" party; we have room for all people of good will! (However, bigots need not apply—perhaps the Republicans have room in their tent that's as narrow as their minds!)

I've been volunteering at the Washoe County Democratic Headquarters for the past few months, helping all the "cow counties" (everything in Nevada outside of Clark County/ Las Vegas, that is!) update the Voter Activation Network (our extremely detailed database). I can't guarantee you that every local Democratic candidate will win in Northern Nevada, but I can assure you that it won't be for lack of organization! The database itself is a marvelous tool that we use to track voter information, including identifying Democratic activists and volunteers. If you are interested in volunteering in any capacity, we will be happy to put you to work!

In mid-January, I also stepped out and tried something new: Canvassing! This entails going door-to-door to talk with people about the issues that concern them (and determining those that don't). Additionally, the canvassing specifically targets non-Republicans who don't vote regularly; you won't confront some rabid Rush Limbaugh "Dittohead." This way, the State Party can identify the "swing" issues that those folks care about, and tailor our message to their concerns. I thought it might resemble visiting the dentist—something you have to do, but no fun. Wrong—I had a blast! Apparently the average canvassing pair knocks on about sixty doors in three hours, and gets about six people to take the survey. My canvassing partner Michael and I did at least twice that many, and we really enjoyed talking with folks about the issues. (FYI, health care, education, jobs, and the economy seem to be hot-button topics, while terrorism, Iraq, and the Yucca Mountain nuclear waste site don't seem to worry these folks much.) The State Party canvasses in Washoe County about once a month;

if you'd like to try it, contact Shannon or Julie at the State Democratic Party Office.

On the national level, I've been watching the Democratic Presidential caucuses and primaries with great interest this season. (Note: I'm biased, having supporting Gov. Howard Dean for months.) All of the candidates have been good on "our" issues (far better than most Republican politicians), but only three supported "same-sex marriage" (Rep. Dennis Kucinich, Rev. Al Sharpton, and former candidate Sen. Carol Moseley-Braun). I liked Rep. Dick Gephardt, but he crashed and burned quickly in Iowa. Sen. Joe Lieberman was an awfully conservative Democrat, and even Vice President Al Gore, who chose Lieberman as his running mate in 2000, didn't support him in 2004; he left the race by early February. Gen. Wesley Clark identified for too long with the Republican Party, and said nice things about Bush until he decided to run for President; he won in Oklahoma before bowing out in mid-February. Two words disqualify Sharpton: Tawana Brawley. I would love to see Kucinich become President, but since he's the most liberal of the lot, that won't come to pass this year. I like Sen. John Edwards, but I don't think he has enough experience (less than four years in the Senate) to be President; he will probably make a good Vice Presidential candidate, if he's willing to accept that role, and can help the Democrats in the South.

That leaves Dean and Sen. John Kerry, the front-runners in this race. (Although Dean may drop out by the time you read this column.) Dean probably expended the most political capital for our community as Vermont's Governor when he approved and defended civil unions, but, to his credit, Kerry voted against President Clinton's despicable Defense of Marriage Act (one of only fourteen senators to do so). Dean's passionate views and demeanor cut both ways, energizing some and alienating others. Kerry, on the other hand, is b-o-r-i-n-g! To me, it's like choosing your life partner: Do you want the guy (or gal) who is solid, and stable, and with whom you have a secure yet passionless marriage, or do you want the guy (or gal) with ideas and enthusiasm who will make some mistakes? Howard Dean's ability to energize voters nationwide reminds me of Bill Clinton. I fear the charisma-free John Kerry won't bring any new voters or enthusiasm to the Party (except those who want to defeat George W. Bush at any cost). Kerry reminds me of "safe" Democratic Presidential contenders like Walter Mondale and Michael Dukakis, who couldn't find a way to connect to non-Democrats, and lost to Republicans in the general election. (By the way, no matter who the Democratic Presidential candidate is, I will support him, and I hope you will, too. I'm not a "yellow dog" Democrat, but I literally WOULD vote for a yellow dog before I would vote George W. Bush for President. For one thing, the dog would probably be smarter!) Intriguingly, in SDNN's February presidential straw poll, Dean received exactly half the votes cast (to 19% each for Kerry and Clark, and 12% for Kucinich), but a candidate needed fifty percent **plus one** for the group to formally him, so SDNN made no official endorsement.

I'm finishing this column the day after the Washoe County Democratic Precinct Caucuses (held, unfortunately, on the same day as the Spectrum Gay/Lesbian Film Festival, resulting in a perplexing choice for many folks). Wow! I wish I could report on what happened in detail inside the auditorium: the presidential candidate speeches; the local candidate speeches; Senator Harry Reid's appearance; the excitement and enthusiasm at the precinct caucus level. But I spent all afternoon trouble-shooting at the precinct registration tables, helping our 40 fantastic, dedicated volunteers get people into the meeting with a ballot, and to the correct precinct (from among about 450 in Washoe County). We expected about 1000 people, and registered over 1500! That's not to mention the work of the eight tireless voter registration folks, who registered over two hundred new Democrats. And we get to do it all over again (but on a smaller scale!) on March 13 at the Washoe County Democratic Convention, to be held at the Atlantis Casino Resort. In Nevada's precinct caucuses, as predicted, Kerry won both Washoe County and the State, but his margin of victory over Dean was smaller in Washoe County than statewide.

On GLBT issues, it's interesting to note that many of the Democratic presidential candidates tried to find a middle ground to grant gay/lesbian couples equal marriage rights without using the words "same-sex marriage" (substituting "domestic partnerships" or "civil unions"). For myself, I don't care if we call it "Green Eggs and Ham," so long as my fourteen-year relationship is treated with the same *gravitas* as that of any other long-standing couple. And thank you, Britney Spears, for recently demonstrating with your fifty-five-hour wedding that the "Defense of Marriage" folks couldn't care less about defending the institution of marriage, as they piously claim; they merely want to hang a "Heterosexuals Only" sign on the chapel door. Probably the most comparable historic situation would be the miscegenation laws that prohibited people from marrying outside their race. While couples won rights state-by-state for about twenty years, the Supreme Court finally put those laws to rest in *Loving v. Virginia* (1967). I believe that twenty years from now, when lesbians and gays are fully integrated into our nation's marriage laws, we will wonder what all the fuss was about. And kudos to new San Francisco Mayor

Gavin Newsom for condoning acts of civil disobedience by permitting gays and lesbians to marry there beginning in mid-February (despite state prohibitions)! How will they get that genie back in the bottle?!

Finally, a lot of hot air has been expended on the issue of a Constitutional Amendment prohibiting same-sex marriage. George W. Bush even mentioned it in his State of the Union speech, to much (deserved) criticism. Such an Amendment will never come to pass. Oh, sure, fundamentalist Republican politicians will thump their chests on this issue, but even they aren't united around how to accomplish it. Keep in mind that both Congressional Houses would have to approve it by a two-thirds majority, and then voters in three-quarters of the states would have to ratify it. If we couldn't pass the ERA by Constitutional Amendment in the Seventies, the American people won't do it on this issue, either. It's clearly mean-spirited and discriminatory; there are too many openly GLBT folks, with too many allies, for this sort of nonsense to pass. If you want to contribute to the effort to fight a proposed Constitutional amendment, follow your heart. But I'm not losing sleep over this issue.

Paul

Blue State

All I have is a page in a dirty magazine. It's not a lot. But I'm proud to be here. And few other people have as much as a page somewhere, so, more than at any other time, here's my shot. My fifteen minutes.

I'm taking on the future of the United States of America. As a columnist, as a voter.

I guarantee I look a little better than Michael Moore.

You've got to be as tired of the 2004 Election as I am. What a hangover! I had to take a Xanax(TM) that night. The months since then have been an ongoing funeral, complete with anger, denial, bargaining, acceptance, and no small amount of beer. We're collectively fastening our seatbelts for a bumpy, barfy ride.

Religion and corporate greed have effectively taken over the United States—with the blessing of the lesser-informed American voters.

That's a strong statement I just made. Are you up for it? I could substantiate it at length, if you want, keeping you way after class. Even if you think that's a bit of a stretch, you must admit that we're in a completely different direction than the America of our youth.

The extreme right is now cemented into power. This will last a minimum of two years. Although things could loosen up again with the 2006 congressional elections, at this point

I'm not willing to place money on it. Worst case scenario, we could be in this for the long haul—a sixty year run of conservativism that makes the Reagan years look like a bad first date.

How and why this has happened is, of course, excruciatingly complex. No matter how you slice it, though, half this country voted ostensibly for a very powerful machine. One that has waged war, weakened our economy, and handed the keys of government over to corporate interests.

It wasn't blue states versus red states. It was city people versus rural people. Educated versus ... well, I'm not going to specifically say "uneducated," but by now most of us have seen the breakout: The states with the highest average IQs voted Democrat; the states with the lowest IQs voted Republican. Right down the line.

But our ability to get fair and balanced information is deteriorating. Nowadays news is like an all-you-can-eat buffet: I choose Bill Maher, The Daily Show, the BBC, and TV5 from France. The next guy may just choose CBN (the news arm of "The 700 Club") and Fox News. And his perspective, therefore, will be totally different. We don't have to be informed, just satisfied. Mainstream news seems intent on just keeping everybody happy.

One of the things the far right wing has laughed at here in the left wing is our undying pessimism. I submit we have to know what's the worst that could happen. So we'll see it coming. And do something about it.

OK, so, what's the worst that could happen? Christian Taliban? Economic ruination? Tanks in the streets? (Specifically, tanks in OUR streets?)

Normally checks and balances keep things in line. Rarely does the balance get so upset that people start dying and systems start to collapse. But we seem to be there now. Healthcare, retirement funds, the environment, personal freedoms, the United Nations, the idea that war is bad .... These ideas are getting phased out in favor of pre-emptive war, Guantanamo Bay, making it legal for companies to dispense with their employees' retirements, and relaxing punishments for high-level corporate law breakers and toxic polluters. Maybe it's because a world out of balance makes more money. Maybe equality, health insurance, and social security programs don't make money. And for that they're being phased out.

Consider a growing idea that the Republicans are only using the Christian extremists because of how much power they provide. The two groups are now feeding off each other, and serve each other's interests, hand in glove. They have become unbelievably powerful.

But did you know that seventy years ago, the devoutly religious were aligned with the Democratic Party? The Democrats were the party of the working man, the union man, the Southern Baptist. The mixture was totally different. This means that nothing lasts forever. Now, though, the poor and disenfranchised are the ones voting for the very same people who want to take away the retirements and cut their wages. We live in a backwards time. Our popular entertainment is based on poking fun of poor people—we make them eat bugs on TV, and we laugh.

Yet ... are these are the people who voted Republican? To stop abortion and gay marriage? Even though their children are being killed in Iraq?

I don't have the data to claim that they are. But I know you've entertained the same thought. No matter what anyone claims, fifty-nine million Americans thought George Bush was on their side. And they don't have to look at information to the contrary if they don't want to.

So where are we? What do we do?

- Take responsibility for getting good and accurate news.
- Educate others when you can, but know that they don't want to be educated. They already think they're right. Take small steps. One-on-one. Don't yell or blame. Listen to them—consider their concerns. Then, later, you'll know how to vanquish their arguments completely. It's rather fun.
- Support organizations that already know what they're doing and know how to fight. Civil libertarians, unions for the separation of church and state. The conservatives rely on huge coalitions, campaigns, pulpits, media and corporations. We need to do the same. Car pool your power!
- Find your bottom line. Know what you're willing to fight for, be it your health care or your own marriage. And be as Norma Rae as you need to be when your time comes.
- Don't be too scared. You're not alone. Every pendulum swing ends sooner or later.
- Know that my next column really is about penises. I promise.

Luke

Play Acting

Ah, my glamorous life in the theater! While I haven't trod the boards in almost twenty years, I had an abiding love for the stage (and the attention, and the applause, and the validation) from childhood.

I began at age seven, with the lead in Antioch (California) Storybook Theater's production of *Rumpelstiltskin*. I was little, cute, and could remember lines—apparently, that was all the training one needed to secure a lead. I continued in several other roles, most memorably as the Cowardly Lion in my second play, *The Wizard of Oz*, a work that still resonates with me. (To this day, my mother believes it was my best role; it's terrible when someone thinks you've peaked at your craft by the advanced age of eight.)

After a few years with AST, I graduated to school productions. I auditioned for the school musical with an *a capella* rendition from *Godspell*. (I had no sheet music or tapes, but I was never afraid to sing.) I remember stunning the junior high choir director, Mary Devine, who decided she had discovered a little star. I was one of only two seventh-graders in the musical *Ask Any Girl*, and I got to sing a duet! By then, I knew I was on my way as a performer.

However, by high school, my father forbade me to take any performance classes; he insisted I fill my schedule with college-prep classes. (I dutifully did so, and finished in the top two percent of my high school class, but then Dad wouldn't sign any of the paperwork I needed to get financial aid for college.) Fortunately, he allowed me to continue performing in high school plays, where I played Radar O'Reilly in *M*A*S*H*, a Southern Baptist preacher in a one-act, and a dancing waiter in *Hello, Dolly!* (*That* performance astounded my mother, who believed I was born with two left feet; she could hardly believe that little asthmatic me was singing and dancing with the other seven guys who performed the Waiter's Galop.)

After high school, I performed in community and church theater groups: Everything from a passion play we performed several times a year during the Easter season (one year we performed on a beach as Easter morning dawned; when I fell in character as a blind man, I inhaled a mouthful of sand, which I spat out while saying my line, probably my most authentic, dramatic performance ever) to an Agatha Christie mystery (as an Austrian burglar who gets killed in the first act) to farce (*No Sex, Please, We're British!*). The latter was the only time I ever broke character; one night, a trowel I threw to the floor in disgust stuck in the wooden stage floor, and swung back and forth like a metronome. All three actors on stage howled with laughter, and we could barely finish the scene.

After my father died in 1982, I could finally attend college, and I decided to pursue a Music degree (having already attained an accounting degree from a business college, and having learned how to type, I could afford to be frivolous in college, since I had developed skills with which I could earn a living). Music majors were expected to perform in California Lutheran University's musical theater productions, so I acted again in a few plays, most notably in our faithful rendition of *West Side Story*, where I played a nameless Jet. (The Sharks were hysterical; every non-WASP male became a Shark. Can you picture several well-fed Japanese Sharks trying to look tough?) Most of our leads were miscast, but the production was a knockout; we Jets received a standing ovation at every performance for our rendition of "Gee, Officer Krupke."

In retrospect, what I always enjoyed most about my performing career was the opportunity it gave me to role-play. Despite my excellent academic performance, I felt very insecure and inferior, mostly because I was gay and didn't want to be. I can identify my sexual/affectional attraction for men to about age four, and I put a name to those feelings by age eleven. However, I didn't do anything about it until I was twenty-three, following my first year of college. As a result, I didn't much like being myself, and I relished the opportunity theater provides to be someone else. Of course, there were several gay kids in Drama Club; the stereotype held fast in my high school. (Drama Club *was* the Gay-Straight Alliance in my day!) But except for maybe one student, no one was out. This was the late 1970s; despite living only an hour's drive from San Francisco, no one I knew was glad to be gay.

This summer, I will have been "out" for twenty years. And it's funny—since college, I have felt no overwhelming desire to act. I sang for several years, but as myself. I wrote a book, but as myself. Did my coming out diminish my need to play other roles, or was it just time to move on? I can't say for certain. There is no shortage of openly gay actors who continue to perform on stage because it's what they were meant to do. But once I felt comfortable in my own skin, I found I no longer needed to hide behind a character's persona. Theatrical performance served as a survival mechanism for me, and I no longer feel the need to validate my existence as a person. Today, in the proud words from *La Cage Aux Folles*, "I am who I am." And that's enough for me.

Paul

Chicago

It was a warm and sultry night. The elevated trains rattled on their tracks, and a humid, almost oppressive feeling hung in the air. People strolled aimlessly, casually bumping and meandering past each other on sidewalks baked by the day's heat. I knew the lingo; every good cop did. Word on the street that night was: Luke wanted to go to a gay bar to get laid.

Strange beasts, gay bars.

Damn, they can ruin your night.

When you're new to 'em, bars can be scary as hell. If you're not new to 'em and you need a nice gin and tonnie just to stop the trembling (sweetie!), then, well, you know all about bars.

Socializing is fine. When you're not actively on the make, a bar can be a great place to hang and have fun.

When you are trying to get laid, though, gay bars take a lot of skill.

When I was young and coming out, the idea of gay bars was deeply frightening to me—as most things were at the time. Then, with practice, I made about as much peace with them as you can make. In my younger days I got passably good at being a witty barfly. (One time I went in to a gay bar in New York City and picked up a trick in ninety seconds flat. He was a very sweet guy with a humongous dick, and when he fucked me I saw the Empire State Building out my hotel window, and knew I was doing all right. It was my very own "Sex and The City" episode.)

But then the internet came along. You know the internet, I'm sure. Chances are I've hit you up on it personally at one point or another. Being online is great. Instead of standing around drinking expensive intoxicants, waiting for someone to stumble into your trap, you can lay around at home watching Star Trek, basically ordering in. And when nothing happens and no one even makes eye contact, there are no witnesses, and bed is just a short commute away.

This sultry night, though, I was out, alone, in Chicago. Trying to work a bar again. Mostly for the hell of it, somewhat just to keep my hand in it. As it were.

Problem is, it's 10 years later. And I look 10 years older, too.

We're damned lucky that we—you and I—aren't fascinated by youth, like most of gay culture. In fact, youth can be a drawback for many of us. In the twink society that most of American gay culture seems to worship, you're hosed after age 35. Those over a certain magical age are forced to spend millions of Euros on the latest twink fashion, trying to dress totally under their age. Are they hoping to fool a 20-year-old into thinking they weren't actually born during the Eisenhower administration?

I shouldn't think it would fool anyone more than does your basic combover. But I like to suck bald men's dicks. I'm not a good person to ask.

So. The bar of my choice was Twink City that night. I'm told that on Sunday afternoons they have an excellent mix of beef and fur. But not for me—the place was packed with the mainstream gay culture. PACKED. I didn't know there were so many of them. And being from San Francisco, I knew no one. So I stood in the corner drinking my beers, forcing myself not to peel the label on the bottles because I've heard it said that label peelers are neurotic.

I saw the same types of characters I used to see in my older bar-going days—here in another city, in another century. Observe:

- The Hit Man: He likes them young, and he'll hit on one, then another, then another, working his way down the line until he finds one who'll talk to him;
- The Aisle Blocker: A flamboyantly witty (in his own mind) queen who's talking wildly and completely blocking the flow of traffic around him, yet he gets huffy, thinking it's the passersby who are the problem;
- The Gods: They know they're hot stuff, and they all stand together. Lesser demi-gods and hangers-on orbit around, streaming off in concentric circles away from the centers of beauty—also blocking traffic;
- The Toilet Wanker: He's at the urinal, you know which guy I mean. Nice dick, actually;
- Normal Partiers: Good-looking, clever, social people drinking with their friends and getting silly with the videos. They actually look good and real, and not like a sappy Zima commercial after all;
- The Shadow: We never know what the deal is with this guy in the dark. He's either an axe murderer or the hottest damned lay in the place;
- The Clothes Horse: It's all '70s and Qiana now. I saw one guy, I swear, wearing Peter Fonda's sunglasses from "Easy Rider"; and
- The Overly Contemplative Bearded Geek in the Corner Smoothing Down His Beer Label: He needs love, too.

For most, a bar is just what it is—a collection of people in a room. Unless you need something. Validation? To get laid? A friend? A place to stay for the night?

Fuck you. You'll get nothing but booze and that awful Kylie Minogue song stuck in your head. "Na Na Na n'na na na NA na ..."

I'm aware that it's possible to ride the wave in a strange place and totally come away with good people, friends, and nipple tugs. But not for me that night. Wasn't in the cards; wasn't in the clientele, probably wasn't in ME. Sometimes you just carry the wrong hope in your eyes.

I stopped by a bathhouse instead. After yet another hour of stomping around glaring at more mainstream gay men, I finally fucked a guy up his butt and went to my hotel alone. I'm probably glad I never saw his face.

Luke

The Summer of '84

Twenty years have passed, but some aspects of the summer of 1984 remain as fresh as if they happened yesterday. I had left home in the Bay Area for college (California Lutheran) in Thousand Oaks in the fall of 1983, and had just finished my first year's studies. (My report card that semester shows a 3.90 GPA in German, Psychology, Music Theory, Piano, Voice, and Concert Choir.) Much as I enjoyed that first year, I struggled emotionally; knowing (but not having acted on) my homosexual orientation for many years, I wanted to experience Love. I roomed in the dorms with three 18-year-old straight boys, while I was the "old man" at the advanced age of 22. Ray, Eric, Robert, and I had little in common, but we all got along fine. Of course, four to a three-room dorm "suite" (with connecting bathroom) provided precious little privacy. But in those close quarters that year, I learned a lot about the emotional lives of young men, about which I previously had no clue.

Still, having completed my first year's studies, I wanted to tackle my sexuality issues in earnest. Earlier that year, I had purchased occasional copies of *The Advocate*, reviewing them feverishly and then discarding them so my roommates would discover no "evidence" of my proclivity. I even drove into Los Angeles (about an hour's drive southeast), trying to find West Hollywood. I knew it centered around Santa Monica Boulevard, but first I went west instead of east off the

405, then I went back the other direction, through Century City. I gave up in sheer frustration at what I now know was the western edge of Boys' Town. So near and yet so far!

Shortly before the semester ended, I had an impromptu chat with Mary Rubin, our Psychology assistant, outside my dorm. For some reason, we were talking about sexuality. With my head bowed, I very timidly remarked that I thought I was probably gay, and Mary piped up, "Of course you are! Everybody knows that!" *What?!* Then Mary told me she was a lesbian. Wow! For my last two years of college, Mary became my best friend—we even lived together the following summer (I slept on the couch in the apartment's living room, while she and her girlfriend took the one bedroom). Curiously, we both developed an addiction to playing bingo several nights a week with all the blue-hairs at the Catholic Church, and she kept me in stitches with her verbal repartee. (And I'll *never* forget the time she answered the phone in the middle of an orgasm!) Mary became my first guide into this scary new gay world, and I remain forever grateful. She even told me she knew I would have a relationship that would last 20 years—and Kurt and I continue to close in on that mark! (However, I lost contact with Mary many years ago. I believe in "six degrees of separation," especially in this community, so if you know her, tell her I'm still looking for her!)

While I originally planned to return home after my first year away at college, a once-in-a-lifetime opportunity presented itself. Los Angeles would host the Summer Olympics that year, and virtually every Southern California college sent singers to participate in the thousand-voice choir for the Opening Ceremonies. When Cal Lu selected me to sing bass, I decided to stay in Thousand Oaks for the summer.

The toughest part of accepting my homosexuality was reconciling it with my Christianity. Mary suggested I attend service at the nearest Metropolitan Community Church, located about half an hour's drive from our home in Thousand Oaks. I was very leery of this—I had heard stories in Christian communities of gay people having sex on the altar and in the pews during services. Mary knew this was untrue, and told me to go see for myself. So one Sunday evening in early June, I drove to the Unitarian Church in Ventura (where MCC held its services). I tiptoed in terrified, and left euphoric. For the most part, the worshipers were gay Christians—an oxymoronic concept to me! Somehow they had reconciled their beliefs and their sexuality; if they could do it, maybe I could too! Toward the end of service, couples approached the altar to take communion together. One couple in particular left a lasting imprint on me because both men were rather homely. After taking communion, they gently kissed. That shattered me! Everything I knew of homosexuality seemed to demand physical beauty. These guys, who would never grace the pages of *Blueboy* magazine, obviously loved each other. Maybe there was more to being gay than just sex—maybe I could fall in love with another man!

A few weeks earlier, Mary and I attended a gay discussion group in Ventura. I was drawn to its leader, a very attractive older man of 48. The next time we went back, June 22, he, Mary, and I were the only ones there. Mary sensed the sexual tension between "John" and me, excused herself, and went home. That night, at age 23, I had my first sexual experience. I felt apprehensive, and nervous, and eager—and thrilled beyond words! While I expected to feel ashamed for expressing my sexuality, the Cheshire-cat grin on my face the next morning revealed my true feelings—screw guilt! The next night, Mary and I celebrated relinquishing my virginity.

As the new young man in church, many of the guys there wanted to get to know me better; I became "popular" almost immediately. Some almost-relationships developed, as did some unwise sexual experiences—"Naïve, party of one!" Fortunately, nothing irreversibly harmful occurred, although I learned about things like open relationships and bisecting love triangles. (As Bette Midler sings, "I was young and—stupid. Hah! Ain't like that no more!")

June ended with the church participating in Los Angeles's Gay Pride Parade. So I finally made my way to the mythical West Hollywood, my new friend Dani Kallio (bisexual female) and all the other MCC folks beside me. Within the space of one month, I went from hiding in the closet to marching in one of the biggest Gay Pride parades in the nation! (I also remember trying to explain to one of the picketing "Christian" protestors why it was OK for me to be gay. It was like teaching a pig to sing; it wastes your time and annoys the pig.) But determining how to live my life with integrity had occupied most of my "free" time since I was 11 years old; I just had to fit the spiritual-sexual piece together before I could come out gay and proud. Now that I had, nothing could stop me. (Clearly, nothing has!)

A few weeks later, I went to an MCC retreat near Santa Barbara, where I met a 46-year-old Cal State Bakersfield professor. Norm became my first lover, in a relationship that lasted all of two months. I thought we would eventually live together, but Norm was married (his wife knew when they married that he was gay, and she knew we were "dating"—it was all very Noel Coward), and he had no such intention. Accordingly, I broke off our relationship shortly after I returned to college in September, but we shared some satisfying moments together.

In July, not only did I participate in the Olympics' Opening Ceremonies, I was also selected to sing at the Closing Ceremonies! I most vividly remember the sheer terror the choir felt during the Opening Ceremonies when we heard what sounded like an explosion directly behind us (originally, an eagle was supposed to fly down from behind us to its trainer, but it died the night before the Ceremonies; someone substituted a man with a jet-pack, but no one told us—even pre-9/11, people worried about terrorism); getting autographs from several of the athletes (including the gold medal-winning male gymnasts; I missed getting Mary Lou Retton's autograph by *this much!*); waiting before the Closing Ceremonies while a giant beach ball transcended language and cultural barriers all the way around the indoor arena, to wild cheers; and dancing in the center of the stadium while Lionel Richie sang "All Night Long." I had the best time, exceeded only by my participation as an athlete in three Olympic-style Gay Games. (Unfortunately, many years later, thieves robbed our home in Phoenix and stole my Olympic commemorative medal; its sentimental value made it the only truly irreplaceable item they stole.)

I also joined the Gay Men's Chorus of L.A. later that summer, and suddenly had 70 new brothers (and a few "sisters" as well!) who played pivotal roles in my coming-out journey. Only two things united us all—our sexual orientation and our love for choral music. In all other ways, I discovered our incredible diversity. With them, I began to learn to let my hair down (metaphorically speaking) and have fun. I had some intense crushes—some requited, some not—and I began to define my role in the community.

What a trip down Memory Lane! The summer of 1984 changed my life irrevocably, and I fondly remember those experiences (even the awkward and stupid ones—sometimes you have to make your own mistakes!). What I learned then still impacts me today. Twenty years after coming out, I continue to discover more about myself and my community, as I hope we all do. And while I'm probably not yet who I will become, I'm definitely not who I was! I hope the same holds true for you.

Paul

Damn He's Ugly

I need to quit banging the Beauty Button in my column, but that's just because I need to quit banging the Beauty Button in my LIFE. Of all the issues I've got, this is the one that keeps coming up again and again and again.

Somehow I keep thinking I warrant a super gorgeous hunky man for my very own.

It's dumb. Am I so beautiful that I deserve one? Honestly? No.

Am I so shallow that, in order for a man to have meaning for me, he must be a bo-hunk?

Um ... I'm working on it.

I watch the circles of beauty around me, here in San Francisco. The A-List. Bearded, hairy, and increasingly loaded with steroided muscles (don't they all seem to know each other?). To them I'm a pest, trying to date way out of my league. You'd think I've seen *Muriel's Wedding* enough to get it by now. But I keep coming back for more.

Beauty is a commodity. It's openly traded in society. You get what you're able to pay for. The currency is your ability to reflect light.

You see, no conversation in the history of the human race has ever started with: "Damn, he's ugly. I'd like to get to know HIM!" So I know it's not just me. We all love pretty people. And muscles. And fur. And a smile that knocks you off your feet.

Because I've been a bachelor for so long, I'm fully conditioned to go by first impressions. When rutting around for dick, we all go for the meatiest, hottest ones we can find. Those fleeting tastes, those curves of thighs, and nasty moments of pleasure are the things we live for. I make no apologies.

Sure, sure, I know, beauty's only skin deep. Can't take it to the bank. Beauty is never frozen in time. Get to know a beautiful man, and he'll cease to be beautiful the first time you see the inside of his refrigerator. Different strokes for different folks, and maybe your idea of the perfect man is one who can bite an apple through a picket fence. I'm a shallow bitch, and I'm headed for nothing but misery. All these things I understand in my tiny little brain.

It's fascinating, though. Beautiful men are pieces of art. They cause a hormonal response in all but the most dead among us.

It's not a gorgeous man's fault that he was born with the birth defect called "beauty." I want to drink of that beauty, and I also want to know: What does this birth defect do to a man's character? I often figure that what I lack in looks and pecs and chest hair can be made up by my quirky intelligence, big dick, and ability to cook.

My mantra: "Let me be the brains, sweetheart. You just stand there and look good forever. And let me hold your hand in public."

Haven't had any takers, but I keep trying.

Sometimes I'll get too burned out, and start hating gorgeous men on sight. That's not constructive; it just gets me bitter inside.

Spazz, total spazz.

And then, just when I think I can never be moved again, I'll see a man. A beautiful man. One who reminds me of what it's all about. How could I not celebrate such form of flesh, such a spirit of light in his eyes? His inability to carry on a conversation will be overlooked as I bask in his beauty and wonder what he eats for breakfast. Will his mom like me? Here just may be a man so cute as to make egg farts between the sheets irrelevant forever!

Then, just as quickly, we run smack-dab into the league problem again. Specifically, that I'm in one league, and Mr. Walking Piece of Art is in another.

Someday I'll learn, once and for all, that real beauty starts out small, and then grows up tall. I'll learn that when I stop being a bachelor and start being a caring human being, all manner of beauty and nuance await me.

Until then, fuck that shit. I want to look at the hot guys. I want to thrill to the possibilities. I want to get inside the gestalt with all the powers of my intellect.

I especially want to sit in the corner and get hurt. Over and over and over again.

While I wait, it's awfully fun to get snarky. I like to picture a documentary on water buffalo as I watch from my vantage point. The image is particularly effective if you're able to imagine the voice of David Attenborough or Leonard Nimoy:

The herd of males, gathered in front of a San Francisco Starbucks Cafe, huddles around the natural formation of caffeine and foamy 'spresso milky froth. Suddenly, a Southern California Behr enters the mix. He's powerful. He's hairy. He's excited and strong; he knows he's going to land high up in the local hierarchy, and he waits for his chance to spread his sperm (or more accurately, to swallow the sperm of the local males).

Observe how the other gorgeous bucks will regard the new arrival. Their curiosity is revealed by shifting their weight, jockeying for eye contact, even blatant primping. Jealousy can be seen, but the primary emotion is one of lust and excitement. The local Alpha Males will vie for attention, but it's clear from the outset that the most attractive local male will win. He has the entitlement—he has the actual title—and he will pair up with the intruder for the first round of mating.

The secondary and tertiary homosexual men will occasionally enter the fray, but they are quickly rebuffed. Their only hope is to occasionally be humored by the Alpha Males as they begin to tweak each other's nipples and issue low "woof" sounds ....

Someday I'll get over it. I'll quit picking on the cute men and leave them to stew in their own social juices. And I'll be happy as a clam, waiting for a true-to-life Mr. Right to pass alongside my picket fence.

Luke

Fahrenheit 9/11

George W. Bush is his own worst enemy, a rocket surgeon if ever there was one. Was he born with that smug, silly smirk? When he feigns sincerity, it's even worse—his eyes are shiftier than a Yugo salesman's. Amazingly, Dubya makes his father, George H.W. Bush—a man who never met a phrase he couldn't mangle, a man deficient in both charisma and vision—appear statesman-like by comparison.

Director Michael Moore begins his documentary by showing us the troubled Dubya in the aftermath of his unprecedented Presidential appointment. Did you know Inauguration onlookers pelted his motorcade with eggs? That Americans never saw coverage of Dubya and company proceeding down Pennsylvania Avenue because they feared for their safety from angry protestors? In his first eight months in office, Dubya excelled only at taking vacations, spending 42% of his time playing golf, and tending to his Texas ranch.

9/11/01 changed Dubya's political fortunes. Moore effectively depicts the tragedy of that day without pictures (but with sound). In fact, perhaps the documentary's most stunning moment comes when, after an airplane pierces the first of the twin World Trade Center towers, an undaunted Dubya proceeds to his photo op at a Florida elementary school. When an aide informs him during the event that a second airplane hit the other tower, and that the nation is under attack, George sits vapidly for several minutes, taking no action whatsoever. (Was he waiting for someone—Vice President Dick Cheney, perhaps?—to tell him what to do?) Moore infers that Dubya was contemplating how to protect the Bin Laden family, as Bush and his retinue had received over $1.4 billion of Bin Laden/ Saudi Arabian largesse over three decades. Accordingly, within days, he and Saudi Arabian Prince Bandar (known as "Bandar Bush" to Dubya's inner circle) decided to link the Afghani Al Qaeda's actions to Iraq (a country with a dictator we disliked) instead of Afghanistan (a country Cheney's former company Halliburton needed to keep a crucial natural gas pipeline running from the Caspian Sea).

Apparently Dubya and his minions also sufficiently understood the psychology of terror to know that by keeping people vaguely afraid long enough—"creating an aura of endless threat"—they will make fearful decisions. How else could Congress pass the "Patriot Act," restricting civil rights and Constitutional freedoms Americans have taken for granted for centuries? Did they read it? Rep. John Conyers (D-MI) kindly (and somewhat facetiously) explains to Moore: "Sit down, my son. We don't read most of the bills. Do you really know what that would entail?"

Dubya evinced no real interest in capturing Al Qaeda's leader Osama Bin Laden, the individual primarily responsible for 9/11, making only feeble, belated attempts toward that end. Instead, on March 19, 2003, the American government invaded Iraq, a country that had never killed an American, or even directly threatened America—"freeing" people who needed no freeing—to provide Dubya his political scapegoat. (Dubya declaims, "We have to bring the ideal of freedom and democracy to [Iraq]." Really? Can't other countries choose their own forms of government? Must America bomb every nation that refuses democracy? How democratic is that?) And pity the (literally) poor, mostly disenfranchised American soldiers who can't understand why the Iraqis don't "appreciate" their efforts, as they terrorize residents in their homes with unannounced middle-of-the-night raids (one says, "They hate us—why, I'm not really sure"; another remarks, "I don't understand it—we're trying to help these people"). Meanwhile, Dubya praises our soldiers while simultaneously attempting to curtail veterans' benefits. But he masterfully protects his constituency: the "haves" and the "have mores"—as he states, "Some people call you the elite; I call you my base." And war proves good for American business, creating seemingly limitless (and arguably unethical) profits for Halliburton and other contractors, thanks to the military's "scorched earth" tactics (destroying Iraq to save it—sound familiar?).

Then there's Lila Lipscomb's story. A Flint, Michigan resident (Moore's hometown) and mother of two soldiers, she speaks of her journey as a "conservative Democrat" from supporting the war and the President to her anguish over her son Michael's death in Iraq in a Black Hawk helicopter crash. Moore dramatically captures a confrontation in front of the White House with an old woman protesting the war (with whom Lila is sympathetic), and a young woman who claims that the moment has been staged (whom Lila proudly faces down).

This Republican administration constitutes a bad bunch, but simultaneously Moore spares neither the mass media (who refuse to hold Dubya, et al., accountable for their lies and misrepresentations) nor the Democrats (portrayed as spineless wimps who fear appearing "unpatriotic") nor the

Senate (not one Senate member would support the many minority Representatives who opposed ratifying the 2000 Presidential election results, as required by law, leaving those results officially unchallenged).

F-911 also provides considerable (mostly unintentional and ironic) humor. Moore notes that the "Coalition of the Willing" against international terrorism includes such powerhouses as Palau, Costa Rica, and Iceland. Attorney General John Ashcroft has a pleasant singing voice. A Congressman licks his comb before running it through his hair. Two Army recruiters in Flint, a city with an unemployment rate near fifty percent, stalk the city's "poor" mall, aggressively attempting to recruit hesitant youth. Thanks to the Transportation Security Administration, an airline passenger may carry up to two lighters and as many as four books of matches onto an airplane in the name of homeland security—boy, do I feel safe!

F-911 probably provides as scathing an indictment against the Bush administration as could be done contemporaneously. Little wonder that despite winning France's Palm d'Or award, Disney refused to release it. Fortunately, someone in Hollywood (Lions Gate) has guts. Dubya desperately wants you to ignore this film; don't do it. No matter your position on the political spectrum, I can't imagine anyone passively viewing this film and taking no action afterwards. Remember come November.

Paul

No.

One of the smallest words in our language is, evidently, the most difficult. Hard to say, and significantly harder to listen to.

This discussion comes in two parts: The value of the word "no," and the degree to which I go to pieces when it's used on me.

Hey, I just write; I don't have to make sense.

As you've certainly noticed, kids don't hear the word "no" at all. I've still got a scar from where I kept sliding down the stairs in a sleeping bag while continuing to ignore the "nos" of one parental unit. Picture Gene Wilder as Willie Wonka: "Please, (yawn), don't, stop ...."

Smack.

"MOMMMM!"

Entire cultures exist where they never really do say no, at least not in polite conversation. It drives up the cost of doing business no end:

"We wanna open a factory here."

"Ah. Factories are wonderful. You are very clever."

"So, when can we start?"

"Ah. You are very clever."

The relevance of the word "no" increases when we include the internet, my constant bailiwick. All we have online are words (words and stunningly misleading pictures). So people clearly need to be more direct. Yet they become less so.

On the internet, to say no, evidently you just ignore a person. It seems to have evolved as a dominant paradigm of internet culture, for good or bad. Yet people still get real huffy, "wouldn't even say anything back to me, how chicken-shit is THAT?"

Well, I think it's fabulous. No confrontation, just a passive-aggressive person's wet dream.

Sometimes we need to hear the word "no," tho. When I'm trying to hook up for sex but the other person isn't into it, they just can't seem to say it. Not even to let me shut up and move on. They say things like:

"Sounds like a plan!"/"Sounds like fun!"

"I bet the fact that you have a big dick means you never go hungry."

"My roommate and I are having popcorn right now."

And my favorite way of saying no: "... the thing is, after so-and-so's party and when we saw each other at the grocery store and ... [eighty seven words later, none of which actually include the word "no"] ... so maybe I hope you understand."

Face-to-face, in a bar, I've heard it's much more difficult to say the word "no." People can be a lot more aggressive in a bar, somehow in direct proportion to their age and apparent ickiness. One night, in a skanky Polk Street bar in San Francisco, this really quite elderly individual in a leisure suit and cigarette—that's how long ago it was!—tried to feel me up, and asked, "Is there money involved?" I was nearly institutionalized from the shock. But I still didn't say no. I just backed off in horror.

(As an intermediate battle tactic in bars, when the word "no" doesn't seem to get through, I've learnt that you can just feign a sexually transmitted disease. Trust me. Shuts 'em right up. But then we're in the "not saying no when we should be saying no" territory once again, and that's not what this is about.)

Years ago I worked for a dirty magazine. Can you bear it? Anyway, I was responsible for crafting a letter to guys who wanted to get naked for us. The answer wasn't always yes. But how do you tackle that? After a month of staring at a blank screen, dozens of inquiries going unanswered, I finally realized that such a letter would have to involve the word "no," and there was no way around it. Once I made that realization, the ideas came quick and I think people's dignity remained intact anyway.

So we need to use the word "no" a lot more often. It can actually be kinder than all the lying and stalling and squirming.

The delivery matters, of course. No reason to be mean about it.

Some people seem to have no goddamned compunction about saying "no," at all, ever.

"Excuse me, is this seat avail—"

"No."

"Hi, I think you and I work in the same building downto—"

"NO!"

I have encountered a few of those: Rejections that are so cruel as to be kinda funny. Like the guy I tried to solicit at a convention to be a famous grrrr-naked model in a very (VERY) prestigious magazine. He interrupted me, handed my business card back to me, flatly stating that I was not his type, and marched off.

You learn to dismiss the ones who say "no" too much as being fart-faces. As you learn to dismiss the ones who WON'T say "no"—even after you give them every permission in the world—as being wimps. Or even control freaks, for if they say "no," you won't keep trying to kiss their ring, will you?

HOWEVER: Part Two.

I Fall to Pieces (Patsy Cline).

Even online, those standard "sorry, not a match" automated rejection notes leave me a tattered mess. I hate it. No one wants to be told no, especially when you're really putting yourself on the line with your heart and soul and buttered butthole.

I can't be alone in that.

But I can tell you than when a kindly "gawd yer hawt but I have herpes right now" comes my way, I do get over it and I wind up with a bit of respect for that person.

So, having said all that, is a greater world of truth and clarity coming to an internet near you?

Probably not. But a man can dream. Dream that you will at least let me know what's on your mind.

That I don't have a chance in hell.

Cuzz then I'd just move on. Eventually. Or at least bargain with myself and say that you're confused and you don't really mean it.

Luke

Wine, Women, and Song

"Too much of a good thing is wonderful." Mae West

In my overly-cautious and faraway youth, one received caution concerning wine, women, and song. (Why song? Did a little jazz ever hurt anyone? Or did musicians seduce one into other temptations? I earned a Music major in college, and I never did anything more dangerous with it than sing in church.) Of course, as a gay man, I replaced the caution toward women with caution toward sex with men. I enjoy it in relative abundance, but I'm not obsessed with or addicted to it. (Others may consider me a sex-obsessed fiend, but that just means they're jealous!) And certainly some wine is fine (in the Bible, the apostle Paul recommends it to Timothy for digestive purposes—1 Timothy 5:23). But whatever drug messages circulated during my formative years resonated with me (thanks, Mom!): In my life, I've smoked exactly one joint (in the storeroom at Karl's Shoes when I was 17 with a high-school classmate and co-worker), and I've never touched a cigarette or ingested anything stronger. However, substance abuse remains a serious problem in our community.

I received a rude shock recently as I watched *101 Rent Boys Uncut*, a documentary produced and directed by Fenton Bailey and Randy Barbato, in which they paid 101 male prostitutes in Los Angeles $50 each to discuss their lives, loves, hopes, and fears on camera. About an hour into the film, they introduced the subject of drugs, and suddenly there appeared one of my former gay tennis circuit buddies. I nearly fell off the sofa! One of the best B division players of my generation, Frank was also one of the canniest strategists I've ever known. I remember that he briefly relocated from L.A. to Phoenix (where I lived at the time) in the late '90s; we played singles together there, and he told me that if I worked on my mental game, I would secure more victories on the circuit. (He was right.) We both worked as legal secretaries, and his friendship and encouragement meant a lot to me. But when Frank returned to L.A., I mostly lost track of him, although I would still scan tournament draws to look for his name. On the rare occasions when he did enter a tournament, he lost quickly and vanished. But I never dreamed his problem could be drug-related (although he suffered some bizarre losses to players I thought he should have defeated easily).

In the documentary, here's what Frank had to say:

My name is Frank McGinnis. And I'm 35 years old. I always shoot up crystal [methamphetamine]; that's my choice. I don't like snorting it, or anything else. It makes me a little worried; I do get a little worried about it. I'm more concerned, believe it or not, about seeing people on the streets than myself. I can't see myself in their same— you know what I mean? I mean, for some reason, I don't see myself as being that, even though I know I'm exactly where they are, you know. I told myself I would never do crystal again if I lost one of my teeth, or whatever, you know. 'Cause it's real common with people losing their teeth, you know. And half my tooth fell out once, and I didn't care. You know, I can go from one bar to the next, without a place to live night to night, with a dime in my pocket most of the time. And live that way. And in between, I go to AA [Alcoholics Anonymous] meetings. [Laughs] You know, and try to get out of it. I played in a tennis tournament; was seeded second in this tournament. And in the middle of the night, I had to go out and get drugs. I could barely even walk the next day. You know. I forfeit a lot of things. Remember that song from Sheryl Crow? "All I Want to Do Is Have [Some] Fun"? That was, like, my theme song for so long. You know. [Sings faintly] "All I Want to Do ..." My friends used to say, "Are you still having fun?" You know what I mean? And I'd say, "Well, I'm trapped." "No, you're not. You can get out of it." I do feel trapped. You know. And it's not even a trap—Before it was a trap I didn't want to be in. Now it's a trap that I don't really care anymore. You know, you get to that point where you just don't really care.

It angered me when I watched that clip, to see such a smart person reduced to such a desperate situation. And it scared me, because it just as easily could have happened to me.

So here's my unsolicited advice: Sing (make music, etc.) all you want. Have all the sex you like, so long as it's safe, and you don't confuse sex with love. But please, please be careful when it comes to substance abuse: too much of a good thing could ruin your life. Or end it.

101 Rent Boys Uncut, Fenton Bailey and Randy Barbato, producers and directors, Strand Releasing, 2001. (Available at www.strandreleasing.com, www.worldofwonder.net, or www.tlavideo.com.)

Paul

Getting To Know You

Now that I'm actually getting to know people, instead of just trying to get into their pants, I got all kinds of crap coming up.

Jaizuss, you people are nuts.

I'm gonna have to ask you all to be nicer. To tricks, ex-tricks, failed tricks and not-on-your-life-would-I-let-you-ever-be-my-trick tricks.

What's with the attitude?

We tend to throw people away the minute something goes wrong. You get to know a guy and it starts all hot and sexy, but then he says, "I'm really into guys whose left testicle is lower than the right, and yours is the other way around so I'm gonna have to let you go now."

Seriously, that's exactly how focused we've become. If a guy comes up short, out he goes, never to be acknowledged again.

In the real world, if you've been to someone's house— even if only once for a few minutes—chances are you'd say "hello" to them if you saw them again in the grocery store.

Not with gay guys. You could have had your tongue up his actual poo-hole, but if you didn't get everything you wanted, you cut 'im dead and look the other way.

How corny is that? (Sorry. Couldn't resist.)

As we begin this discussion, know that I'm still not getting it right. But I'm trying. You can try too. It's not so hard to be nice. Just to say "hi." Give a little acknowledgement out there.

Nodding and saying "hello" does not obligate you to anything. It just makes the world a better place. I often see a guy in my neighborhood, he doesn't fit in really. He and I have very little to say to each other. But he comes out to the Castro in his little car, and I began to realize that having someone acknowledge him and say "hi" to him is probably the highlight of his day. You could just sit back and say he's a sad person, if it helps you. Or you could be less of a prick.

One of the biggest reasons we cut people dead, I think, is because we don't want them to get "the wrong idea." If we're not interested in sex with a person, then any scrap of attention you give might fire up their lust again. It could be just gross. And you certainly don't want that to happen. Another guy I know in the Castro is kinda sexy to me, and I've indicated I'd like to check him out better. Well. Clearly the answer is no: When he sees me, he gets so busy tossing his head, avoiding eye contact with me, I honestly fear he's gonna throw out his neck. Now I mostly wanna go up to him and say, "Chill, dude, I get it. Take it easy on your spinal column, or you'll give yourself scoliosis …."

If not sex, then … must it be nothing? Can we function on no other level? For some people, maybe not. Can you? Ask yourself that if you want to come out and be with us in the real world. You may be a little more tired than you think.

This is all on the trick level so far. Easy come, easy go.

What if you actually have feelings for a man? What if he cuts you dead because he REALLY doesn't want you to get the wrong idea? As your Master and Columnist, I don't have an easy answer for you—here at *100% Beef*, you always get a free existential morass to go with your porn—but let me tell you about two men I know who illustrate this problem. In case it helps.

The first is Mark. Mark is actually beautiful. Heart-stoppingly cute. And shy! He knows how much I want him, and it puts him off. Plus, he's married to a gorgeous body-builder, let's not forget that. He'll be polite to me—he doesn't completely cut me dead—but clearly he doesn't know what to do with me. Every once in a while he'll throw me a scrap, we'll have a clever conversation, and I'll come away feeling wonderful. Does this mean he might let me do him? Yeah, that old hopefulness fires right up: One point for the "ignore them if you don't want to do them" crowd. But on another level, I actually like talking to him. Thoughts of his naughty bits get mixed with something more touching. Would I have him as a friend if that's all I could get? I'd still get to look into those amazing eyes of his, and hear what he has to say. Maybe if I stopped trying to dry-hump him he would finally see I'm not so much of a putz after all.

The second man is Mike. After three dates and no sex, he decided that we were to be "sisters." I don't recall getting to vote on that, and I was pretty disappointed. But we are pals; now that I've seen how he works, I know it's same with every other man he meets: Rapid sisterhood, with or without an initial roll in the hay. Yet he's openly looking for his Mr. Right. Do I sound like a stalker if I still think it could be me, once he settles down? Again: I don't try to get into his pants anymore. I just listen and try to be a friend.

In both cases, I could have told these guys to go to hell because I'm not getting what I want. And maybe someday I finally will. But I'm not ready to throw them away because they seem to be quality people. I look good standing next to quality people.

For the besieged and constantly hit upon out there: Be firm and consistent, but GENTLE. Don't throw people away just because they want to smell your underwear.

For the horny: Stand-down from boner alert. If the answer's not an immediate "yes," then it probably means the answer's a forever "no." Listen instead for what else might be waiting for you: A friend. You never know, some of his other friends could be fuckin' hot. And then you can start the process all over again.

Luke

How Can 59,054,087 People Be So Dumb?*

GLBT folks (and Democrats and progressives) would sooner forget November 2, 2004, although we can ill afford to. John Kerry failed to unseat "King George" (Bush), who believes that receiving 51% of the popular vote grants him a "mandate." The virtually unchanged status of "red" and "blue" states since the 2000 election (Bush lost New Hampshire but picked up New Mexico) demonstrates the stalemate between urban and rural America. One humorist recommended dividing the U.S. into two countries—one for Democrats, one for Republicans—which begins to sound sensible.

Despite my being a passionate, committed Democrat, I preferred former Vermont Governor Howard Dean to candidate Kerry. But I discovered I underestimated him: *Newsweek* reported that in a conversation with Bill Clinton, Clinton "urged Kerry to back local bans on gay marriage. Kerry respectfully listened, then told his aides, 'I'm not going to ever do that.'" Bill Clinton wanted to sell out my community for political expediency—Kerry stood with us on principle. John Kerry, I apologize for misjudging you.

Meanwhile, voters passed "Defense of Marriage Act" laws in all eleven states where they landed on the ballot. Despite these laws' blatant unconstitutionality, if Dubya appoints new

Supreme Court justices (as expected), the Court that gave gay people Constitutional rights last year could be replaced with one that takes them away next year.

And what issue facing our nation proved most important to voters? The war in Iraq? The war on terrorism? Health care; education; jobs; the economy? Try "moral values." Out in the red states, conservative (Republican) Christians hate us baby-killing, bra-burning, queer-loving, liberal (Democratic) atheists. I'm a Christian, but these fundamental extremists make me almost ashamed to be one.

Fewer Democrats will occupy the Senate (from 48 to 44). Even Senate Minority Leader Tom Daschle lost his seat (Nevada's senior Senator Harry Reid will likely assume that position). And fewer Democrats will occupy the House (from 205 to 200). (Fortunately, enough Democrats remain in each branch to veto and/or filibuster successfully.)

A few bright lights shone that dark day. Barack Obama, born of an African-American father and a Caucasian mother, became Illinois Senator (defeating black anti-gay conservative Alan Keyes). And Cincinnati repealed its discriminatory anti-gay Article XII with 54% of the popular vote. But bad news clearly outweighed good.

So what's next for the Democrats? Should they select a more liberal, progressive candidate in 2008 to energize the Democratic base (at the risk of alienating moderates)? Or should they choose a Southern moderate (who may opt to "throw us from the train" because we don't possess the proper "moral values")? Kerry likely won't run again. Senator Hillary Clinton has the inside track, but I can't see her turning red states blue (except, perhaps, Arkansas). Dean still has the ear and heart of "the Democratic wing of the Democratic Party," and worked hard on behalf of its ticket despite losing in the primary.

And what's next for the country (especially "cultural minorities")? Optimists believe Dubya will ponder his place in presidential history, and will govern from nearer the center of the political spectrum. However, I see no evidence to support that view, especially given Bush's perceived "mandate" from his ultra-conservative base. Pessimists fear the next four years will likely damage reproductive and gay rights, as conservatives erode or eliminate Constitutional protections, and encourage discrimination in state and local laws. Daring to express what many fear to verbalize, Rod Abid wrote on Advocate.com, "Barring some major change, the Republican Party is setting the table to run this country for a long time to come. And we in the gay community are not invited to sit at this table. ... Among the things that are possible: sodomy laws reinstituted, partnership rights revoked, adoption rights taken away, harassment overlooked by law enforcement. And forget teaching in public schools, or serving in the military. The Republican Party as an organization wants us back in the closet. ... And once the Supreme Court has five votes in favor of this invisibility, our legal rights will be in real and immediate peril."

I keep envisioning Nazi Germany in the 1930s, where gay people's rights slowly improved for three decades, only to be exterminated during Hitler's reign of terror. Will our government forbid us to hold certain jobs (such as teaching)? Will the state prohibit churches from recognizing our holy unions? Will thugs destroy gay institutions, and burn our books? Will America place recalcitrant lesbians and gays in "relocation camps"? I scoffed at the mantra that "this is the most important election of our lifetime"—I've heard that about every single election in my lifetime! But in hindsight, it may be true; I've been out as a gay man for over twenty years, and I've never felt so afraid.

Fortunately, if historical patterns hold, Bush will shoot himself in the foot with a serious second-term scandal, and the Democrats will make inroads in the House and Senate in the 2006 mid-term elections. But that won't happen unless Democrats and progressives vote as if their lives depend on it. That's not hyperbole—that's fact.

* Front-page headline of London's *Daily Mirror*

Paul

"This Column Will Self-Destruct"

Gay men are catching HIV on purpose now.

Having it seems much better than not having it.

And sometimes I agree.

This is a dangerous column. Things are happening here that no one dares mention, and by bringing it up, I might be making it worse. But this is how things are. Not how we wish they could be.

For so many gay men in San Francisco, HIV is no longer a death sentence. It's not really even much of an inconvenience. What it is, though, is license to never have to worry about it again. It's permission to get an ass full of cum at a party with no more concern than that some might queef back out on the subway ride home.

If you think I'm lying, or that only a stupid person would allow himself to seroconvert to HIV, then I salute you. You're safe and sound, and your world makes sense. Congratulations.

It's not that way for everyone, though.

We're in a depraved and twisted time. Modern medicine has made Western cases of HIV manageable. Almost always ....

The pills become fewer and safer, the death sentence feels lifted. Not so, obviously, in Sub-Saharan Africa or for people who have no health care, but fuck them—this is about privileged American homosexuals wanting to get it on and never pay the price.

We just might not ever have to. Maybe.

Oh, we all hear of bug-chasers and barebacking, and we shriek in horror and put up a good front.

Then we stick it in someone without a condom, and it's OK because we promise to feel guilty about it afterward.

HIV-positive men don't use condoms with each other. We bareback. Almost exclusively. Do we get multiple strains of the virus? Super-HIV?

No scientist can accurately answer the question, so obviously I won't try to, either. But I can tell you that the HIV I originally caught in 1996 has remained genetically unchanged in my body, even though less-healthy and more untreatable strains have been fucked into me. Do I recommend that you go out and try? Of course not. One thing is certain: If you get infected with a difficult-to-treat version of the virus, you will have a hell of a battle on your hands. They're out there, the multiple-drug-resistant strains.

Yet when you read stories in the newspaper about Super-Infection, read them carefully. What do they say? And what do they NOT say?

Nobody wants to be responsible for causing a picnic.

Yes, I said "picnic."

Here in San Francisco, men don't really seem to die of HIV-related illnesses anymore. We're back to heart attacks and liver disease. Wonderful news! But men are letting down their guard.

Are bug chasers vastly different from Type II Diabetes chasers? Ill-advised, yes, but you take a few pills and the Pepperidge Farms continue to dance alluringly before us.

We eat of the cake, richly. And everything seems OK.

Yet another friend of mine converted to HIV this morning. Or at least today he found out. He sounded surprised and shocked—I don't know why, because he certainly worked his ass off to get it. He played the "I just won't let guys cum in my ass" game. It took two years, but he finally got a High Score.

Conversely, I was with a friend when he found out that he was still HIV-negative. *And I felt sorry for him.* Because six months later he's going to be right back there all over again, waiting for that shoe to drop.

To be honest, I'm glad I was spared this decision. When I caught HIV nine years ago, it was an honest-to-gawd accident. Broken condom. Protease inhibitors and effective drug cocktails had just come into use back then, and their viability was by no means certain—and when they *did* work, they scarred your body. So my HIV diagnosis was a shock and a defeat. Without pills, I would have been dead by 2001.

We forget what it was like back in the 1980s. So many men died. And they died horribly. Untreated HIV is cancer and starvation and raving lunacy all rolled into one, and twenty thousand gay men—men just like you—shat themselves to death in this prissy little city.

I met Nurse Barbara a few weeks ago at the bedside of a friend fighting cancer—he has HIV, but that's old news; just a background to more pressing concerns. Barbara was an HIV nurse all through the '80s and '90s. She saw it all. And she didn't stand back or hide or turn cold. She wiped our brows, changed our diapers, went to our houses, and vowed she'd never turn her back on us. She's an oncology nurse now. We spoke quietly while Little Jeffy slept the aching sleep of the chemo patient, and she told me about giving a dying man a little stuffed ferret to hold. She said he named it T-Cell, claiming everyone should have at least one in their life. And he died soon thereafter. Barbara cried a little in front of me, fiddling with the stethoscope in her pocket.

Men so rarely die of HIV now that the old wards have been closed.

The nurses have moved on, clearly still hurt by the horror they were forced to watch. I'm glad they still seem to care, even though, apparently, we don't.

So where does that leave us? What will the consequences be of our behavior?

Work continues on an actual vaccine. This would be the perfect solution, because then everyone can resume fucking in a consequence-free environment.

In the meantime, super strains could pop up and kill us all. The pills could stop working. The economy could collapse, and the pills would no longer come.

An even more likely danger, I think, is a political backlash against the homosexuals who stopped caring.

If we don't give a shit, I can promise you mainstream American culture won't, either.

Luke

Elegy for Mumsy

Wednesday, February 2, 2005

Yesterday, after discussing it for several days, Kurt and I decided to put Mumsy down on Saturday. Mumsy, our "eldest daughter," would be 19 in April. Of course, she's a cat. Kurt's had her longer than he's had me (15-1/2 years); he found Mumsy as a stray when he lived in Tempe, Arizona, and she sort of adopted him. She was mothering her first litter of kittens when Kurt found her, and her name quickly metamorphosed from "Mom" to "Mumsy." Kurt theorized that she had been abused and abandoned; Mumsy had excellent house manners, but was very skittish with us at first, and cowered a lot. Over time, she learned to trust and feel safe with us. Once she became comfortable with us, she became the best "lap kitty" ever. (After observing for 13 years, her "baby" sister Punkin is finally practicing the art of lap sitting. Unfortunately, Punkin is twice Mumsy's size, so it's more like having a ten-pound furry barbell sit on your lap. But we adjust.)

However, in her later years, Mumsy spent a lot of time at the vet's, receiving attention for various ailments. She's deaf and blind, but we've lived with that knowledge for several months. Now, however, she's losing her balance, walking around in circles aimlessly, becoming incontinent, and failing to clean herself. (She used to preen in the sun for hours.)

Today, when I returned home from my workout, I heard her mewling, and found her trapped behind the washer, her back legs caught between the hoses and the electrical cords. After extricating her, I knew we were doing the right thing. But it's hard for both of us. We joke about our "lesbian daughters," but Mumsy and Punkin are our immediate family. While I've taken her for granted at times (and I'm really not a "pet person"; I hate for living things to depend on me, even plants), she's a good kitty.

I don't know how much of my grieving is for Mumsy, how much is for us, and how much may be misplaced for my grandmother, who, at 88, has been in a nursing home for several years now. My mother visits her almost every day, but I don't want to remember her that way. I prefer to remember my happy, funny, healthy "Nana." I want to remember Mumsy as a frisky, curious kitty, but at age 43, I know it's important for me to look death squarely in the face. While I've lost a lot of people, I've never dealt with death this close. And knowing that I'm helping to decide when to put her down makes it especially painful.

Friday, February 4, 2005

I'm in the worst mood today. Problems at work; problems with the transcription for my second book. My feet are sore; I'm tired. I have a mountain of work ahead of me (although I'm making progress). And in less than twenty-four hours, Mumsy will be dead.

While I was petting Mumsy yesterday, I thought that maybe what bothered me most is that she has no idea what's coming; she trusts Daddy Kurt and me completely. I really do believe in euthanasia, for people as well as animals, when it's the most humane thing to do. But it's extremely difficult to make that decision on someone else's behalf. When is the right time? What if the manifesting symptoms are only temporary? What if she has six more good months left in her?

Sad, angry, tired, confused – I'm a mess.

Saturday, February 5, 2005

I got up early this morning to spend some extra time with Mumsy before we bring her to the vet's. Her spirits appeared good; in fact, since the washing machine incident, she has seemed considerably better. When I got in bed last night, I asked Kurt if he had seen her improvement. He admitted he had, but that it was just a matter of time. He quoted his father, a physician: "Are we preserving life, or are we postponing death?" We agreed to keep our appointment.

On the way to the vet's, Mumsy meowed a few times; did she sense what was coming? At the vet's, a technician took us into a waiting room, and asked if we wanted a ceramic print made from Mumsy's paws; Kurt declined. While waiting for the vet, I asked Kurt about how Mumsy came to adopt him. He began to tell me, and my stoic yet tender-hearted husband began to cry. I took his hand, and let him talk for a while. When the vet came in, she explained that she was going to give Mumsy a strong sedative, and then bring her back in with us; sometimes, especially when the cat is weak, that itself will bring about its demise. Dr. Kingery took Mumsy, and Kurt and I talked about her some more. When Dr. Kingery brought Mumsy back, partially wrapped in a towel, Kurt held her, while I stroked her head. The sedative slowed her heartbeat and breathing, but she was still alive when Dr. Kingery returned about ten minutes later. So Dr. Kingery placed her on the table, and gently injected an overdose of anesthetic into her left front leg. Within thirty seconds, our baby drifted out of this world. Kurt and I tried to be brave, but we both choked and teared up; neither of us had ever put down a pet before. Kurt removed her collar, and we took it with us in the empty pet carrier. We chose to have Mumsy cremated, and Dr. Kingery said that we should have the cremains in about ten days. When we left the holding room, I heard Sarah McLachlan's "Angels" on the waiting room radio. I've always liked the song, but now its chorus will forever remind me of our good girl:

> In the arms of the angels
> Far away from here
> From this dark, cool hotel room
> And the aimlessness that you feel
>
> You were pulled from the wreckage
> Of your silent reverie
> Here, in the arms of the angels
> May you find some comfort here

Afterwards, we ran some errands, but it's awfully profound to watch anything die, no matter the circumstance. Dr. Kingery was extremely gentle and thoughtful with us; how do you repay that sort of kindness? Then we came home to Punkin. I think she'll be thrilled for a while to have the house (and her electric heating pad) all to herself, but she may be confused later, when Mumsy doesn't come back home.

Should we get a "replacement" cat? Mumsy hissed at and ignored baby Punkin for about a year (before they became constant companions and best friends)—would Punkin continue the cycle? Plus, Punkin's pretty set in her ways; would she want a little sister, or should we just let her be an "only child" now? We've spent a lot of money on vet bills, medicines, special foods, cat-sitting, etc. over the years. I think it's too early to decide; Kurt and I will probably discuss it later.

Tuesday, February 8, 2005

While driving home from work on Sunday night, I heard "Angels" on the radio, and had to turn it off; the wound was still too fresh.

People have been incredibly kind to Kurt and me. Almost everyone has a story about putting down a pet. While intellectually we know ours is not an unusual occurrence, sympathy does ease the pain. Kurt already put away Mumsy's food and water dishes—just seeing that empty space hurts. And I think Punkin knows her sister's not coming back; she's been very melancholy, even for her.

Last night, we went to PETsMART to get some new food for Punkin (Mumsy had a restricted diet; Punkin would eat anything in either her bowl or Mumsy's, so we gave them the same food). While there, we looked at "cat condos" that might encourage Punkin to get more exercise, but we decided to hold off for a while. PETsMART also had a couple of cats up for adoption; we looked, but didn't inquire.

While I miss Mumsy, I'm glad I don't have to worry about her any longer. I believe we did the right thing, and she departed this world as peacefully as possible. But our house feels emptier without her. Now I think that if a tree falls in the forest, even if no one hears it, it still must make a sound. Despite our long, bright garlands of friends and loved ones, Mumsy's (timely) passing snuffed out one little candle in both our hearts.

Paul

Double Doors

A man named Jeff Cochran died in my arms a couple of weeks ago. His heart stopped beating while my hand lay upon it. I felt its last beat—later than it should have been, but no more remarkable than all the rest.

Wasn't supposed to go that way at all; he was only 42.

In my last column, I spoke of a friend in the hospital with cancer. That was him: Little Jeffy. We thought he was going to come out of the chemo and be just fine. He and I had a lot of Sunday beer busts at the Lone Star Saloon yet to do together.

I guess the planet had other plans.

This would be a fairly non-cheerful thing for me to talk about here on your dime. But it's what happened. If I wrote about something else, I wouldn't really give a rat's ass about it, and you'd be able to tell.

You'll get your money's worth.

I write to clear my head; to tell you what I saw.

And to tell you about Jeff. For, like each human who has gone away before him, all that remains are thoughts and memories. Even his voice, which was pretty damned sexy, only exists when I clear my head and remember it. For a while afterward I could call his cellphone and listen to his voicemail greeting, until Verizon shut it off.

Since Jeff was my friend, I can tell you firsthand about all the love he wanted to feel in his heart, and how it didn't matter anymore when that heart stopped beating. His life was modest, his stories of romance were frustrated. He liked country music, dancing, drinking cheap beer from the bottle. He always hoped for more, going to school when he could afford it, and bailing back out when he couldn't. Turns out he wrote poetry no one knew about until we found the books in his apartment.

He wanted to find love. I even helped him look for it a few times, in the sand during a bonfire at the beach.

But I wasn't his lover. Just a friend, after all.

I really don't know how to write a column about all this. I mean, I keep thinking of that episode in "Friends" when Phoebe sings The Grandmother Song to the children:

> *Well lately she hasn't been coming to dinner;*
> *And the last time you saw her she looked so much thinnerrrr?*
> *Well, your mom and your dad said she moved to Peru;*
> *But the truth is, she died, and someday you will too, la la la*
> *la la ....*

Yeah. I got a lotta nerve writing about death in a place like this.

Maybe the subject isn't so far removed as we like to think, though. Looking at sexy naked men in a magazine is a part of sex, and sex is what we do to create life. That palpable thrill you feel in your stomach when you look at a beautiful man is your body wishing to make babies. (The next time you make love, try connecting with the fact that you're actually breeding the man you're with. It will probably blow your mind just a little bit. And that's good!)

Then there's the other end of the spectrum. Death is not sexy in the least, BOY can I attest to that right now. The fear and loss and pain are like a slap in the face. The ANGER of it takes your own breath away. It pretty much fucks you up. You feel old. You feel young. Or you feel nothing at all, and simply want a sandwich. You're as liable to burst out laughing as you are to cry. For two days I actively wished to pummel some or another guy with my clenched fists, preferably while fucking him up the ass. And in this town I probably could have found a willing participant if I thought I could tolerate bruised knuckles and having my iPod stolen.

The death of a friend makes you hug your kitty cat pretty damned tight. Even more surprisingly, Kitty seems to know and doesn't mind.

It's one of those rare moments where all the crap in the world—the Visa bills, the job, who said what to whom—all gets burned off with a blowtorch. You're still there and your friend isn't, and you know this happens every, every day.

The people I truly admire in this world seem to be able to incorporate it all together: They remember the tang of horror just as much as the thrill of forgetting. And they know to laugh either way.

Ed was there, too—another friend at Jeff's side that night. Thank god. We both did this together.

At 11 pm, Jeff would still suck on the little wet mouth sponge, and I'd stroke his head and tell him he was doing such a good job, that we were all so proud of him. At 12:42 am, there was no Jeff at all.

"Yeah. He's gone," said nurse Christiana quietly, folding yet another stethoscope back into yet another smock pocket.

The next time you buy a new shower curtain at Walgreens and hang it on the rod, I want you to remember its smell. You'll meet that smell again someday.

Ed and I rode with him in the elevator down to the Big Double Doors in the basement. That was my idea. I didn't want Jeff to go downstairs alone. I'm not sorry we escorted him, but it was nothing like "CSI." No chrome, no recessed blue neon lighting and swirling dry ice smoke. Just a walk-in refrigerator, thankfully unoccupied when we got there.

We were numb. It was 2:30 am, two days after Christmas. Nothing to do but go home.

I found a parking ticket on my car anyway, outside the hospital. The world didn't care.

By the time my clock rang at 3 am, I was snug in my bed under the covers all warm, while the man I knew—and whose body I'd made love to—was surrendering his warmth forever in a refrigerator.

Kitty didn't only get squeezed, he got damned dribbly wet, too. And still he took it. He knew.

Go pump your iron. Be as snide as necessary to get through the day.

Hug your kitty.

Make love to a man.

We truly have it all.

Luke

U.S. Supreme Court Overturns Sodomy Laws

On the morning of August 3, 1982, Michael Hardwick engaged in consensual mutual oral sex in the bedroom of his Atlanta home with an adult, male, married schoolteacher friend from North Carolina. Hundreds of thousands of U.S. couples, in same-sex and opposite-sex pairs, likely enjoyed the same activity that day. However, Atlanta police officer Keith Torrick, personally serving a public drinking warrant on Hardwick (invalid because Michael had timely paid his fine), walked into Hardwick's home unannounced to the couple, and watched the men from Michael's bedroom doorway for as long as forty-five seconds before Michael identified Torrick's presence: "When I looked up and realized he was standing there, he *then* identified himself. He said I was under arrest for sodomy. I said, 'What are you doing in my bedroom?'" The officer arrested both men and brought them to the Atlanta jail, where they were paraded around for twelve hours; guards pointedly announced to everyone that Michael "was in for cock sucking." Recounting the situation, Hardwick told *Advocate* writer Richard Laermer, "I kept thinking I was about to get gang-banged, and I was scared to death. Because they were letting everyone know that … here's some fresh meat."

The North Carolinian paid a fine and never spoke to Michael again. In a 1990 *Advocate* article, Hardwick said, "I just wanted to go home and forget the whole thing. But this group of [civil liberties] lawyers contacted me and told me they wanted to try it as a test case. They asked me to sit down and write about my experience—the whole thing, beginning to end. I wrote for ten hours nonstop, and that was when I really harnessed my anger. I knew then I couldn't walk away." *Bowers v. Hardwick* became the definitive Supreme Court case that, from 1986 until the Supreme Court overturned all federal and state anti-sodomy laws in 2003's *Lawrence v. Texas,* advanced the proposition that no Constitutional right to privacy existed for gays and lesbians, even in their own bedrooms with consenting adults.

Since federal courts determine constitutional issues, Hardwick's attorneys brought suit before the Eleventh Circuit Court of Appeals; there, on May 21, 1985, a three-judge panel decided in Michael's favor in a split decision. Presiding Judge Frank M. Johnson, Jr.'s opinion stated, "the Georgia sodomy statute implicates a fundamental right of Michael Hardwick. The activity he hopes to engage in is quintessentially private and lies at the heart of an intimate association beyond the proper reach of state regulation." Ruling that both the Ninth and Fourteenth Amendments protected Hardwick's right to engage in consensual sodomy, the Court of Appeals remanded the case to U.S. District Court for trial, requiring the State of Georgia to "prove in order to prevail that it has a compelling interest in regulating this behavior and that this statute is the most narrowly drawn means of safeguarding that interest."

Undaunted, the State of Georgia appealed the suit to the Supreme Court, who heard the case on March 31, 1986. On June 30, the Court released its 5-4 ruling that the United

States Constitution did not include homosexual sodomy under its privacy rights (the Court chose to avoid the issue of heterosexual sodomy). Justice Lewis Powell proved the "swing vote" on the case. Originally siding with those justices who believed the Constitution protected people from interference regarding private, consensual acts conducted in their own bedrooms, Powell ultimately decided that because Atlanta police never actually prosecuted Hardwick for his acts, no harm had been caused, and he sided with the majority against Hardwick. A friend's revelation of the Supreme Court's decision stunned Hardwick: "When he told me, I couldn't believe it. I thought … 'God, it was all for nothing.'" As long-time gay journalist Randy Shilts aptly set the Court's ruling in context,

> *Bowers v. Hardwick* had a devastating impact on the future of all litigation pertaining to gay rights. From now on, whenever a federal court ruled on a gay employment discrimination case, judges hearkened back to *Bowers* as the one Supreme Court precedent on the issue. If homosexuals did not have the right to engage in sex, what right did they have to be exempt from employment discrimination? When gays in uniform appealed their jail sentences on constitutional grounds—and more gays than ever would be imprisoned in the years ahead—military courts invariably pointed to *Bowers* for judicial support to confinement. In thousands of ways every day in the years ahead, the liberties of gay Americans would be circumscribed by the words of *Bowers v. Hardwick*.

What happened to Michael after the Supreme Court decision? He went on "The Phil Donahue Show" (an *Oprah* precursor) to talk about the case ("Up until then, I'd been denying my own homophobia"), returned to bartending and the culinary arts, and created visual art (describing himself as an "optical alchemist").

Hardwick's vindication arrived both on November 23, 1998, when the Georgia Supreme Court struck down its sodomy law in *Powell v. Georgia*, finding that such a law "manifestly infringes upon a [state] constitutional provision ... which guarantees to the citizens of Georgia the right of privacy," and on June 26, 2003, with the U.S. Supreme Court's sweeping reversal of the nation's remaining sodomy laws (in twenty-four states). Sadly, both verdicts came too late for Hardwick, who died from AIDS-related causes in Gainesville, Florida on June 13, 1991.

Michael Hardwick didn't ask to be a gay hero, but personally confronted with an unjust law at the literal threshold of his bedroom door, he didn't flinch from the controversy and the accompanying limelight. In so doing, he served as yet another link in the chain toward American gay sexual freedom stretching from Dale Jennings in 1952 to John Geddes Lawrence and Tyron Garner in 2003. I owe a debt of gratitude to these and many other brave pioneers, even—especially— those who would not live to see the fruits of their labors.

Paul

History

Because it's 2006, we like to think we're the bleeding edge of everything. Our pain is real. Anyone dumb enough to have lived before now just didn't know shit. Don't matter, dead and gone, boring as fuck.

History? Oh please, we're so plugged in! We know the earth is round. We had September 11. We can update our blogs from the comfort of high-speed trains and look up anything we want to learn by a simple right click.

Yet over the years of my own history I've learned I'm a bit of a turn-of-the-century kind of guy. Not this century. The last one. Oh, I love HDTV and antibiotics, but I'll occasionally lose myself researching how to illuminate a home with gaslight, or bone up on how to crank-start a Ford Model A (retard the spark magnetos, and watch out for crank recoil). I'll just do it on my Treo 650 while waiting for a plane.

History is not boring.

History is people who wanted just as much from life as I do—only they're not alive anymore.

Think about 9/11. Despite the numbness and shock you probably felt, you were most definitely, painfully alive that day.

History is how you felt that morning.

For our grandparents it was the attack on Pearl Harbor. For their grandparents it was Fort Sumter and the American Civil War. Just as painful, just as out of context and shocking.

We don't have a monopoly on fear and pain. On December 7, 1941, everyone here was certain Japanese submarines had *already* taken up positions in America's West Coast ports. Attack was imminent. My grandfather, a police officer, was sent to guard Seattle's Piers 90 and 91. Alone. All night long, with only a revolver to fend off the whole of the Imperial Navy. I'm glad I listened to him tell the story—not just facts, but the feelings, too. It was the longest, scariest night of his life.

History is usually about disaster. (We know drama.) I've been a Titanic buff for decades, and I can assure you the Titanic was a pretty bitchin' piece of equipment. The Best.

Yet if Titanic had never hit its iceberg, the ship and everything we know about it would have just been retired. Scrapped and forgotten. It's only because something happened that everyone has fought ninety years to capture every bit they could from that moment. Along with the trivia, we come away with records of what clothes, food, and music were like then. What their thoughts and hopes were. Even what was served at dinner that night. I don't eat turtle, personally, but you go right ahead.

Just as a counterpoint, consider this: At the Titanic inquest, crewman Harold Lowe was asked to repeat someone's use of the word "hell" verbatim—and it was so scandalous they nearly had to clear the courtroom. Compare that with Jerry Springer any day of the week.

And as luxurious as Titanic was, they didn't have hot running water in the cabins. So what do YOU think her captain, the beefy white-bearded E.J. Smith, really smelled like?

See? There's something for everyone in history.

Do you like kinky sex and the Marquis de Sade? Go for it. Look to history.

Sports? Can't imagine personally, but it's all written down somewhere. *Go Spartans!* (No. Literally—Go Spartans!)

They found two thousand year old graffiti in Pompeii a few years back:

"Lovers, like bees, enjoy a life of honey," after which someone else scrawled, "you wish ...."

"Artimetus got me pregnant ...."

"Daddy Colpius kisses ladies where he shouldn't ...."

Don't you totally want to know what Daddy Colpius looked like? But disaster froze that city in time.

When looking at old photographs of men unsmiling and uncomfortable in their stiff collars, I picture them named Kevin and working at Oracle. Some of them are kinda hot. Put 'em in a baseball cap and Krispy-Kreme T-shirt, and they're no different than guys you see at the Lone Star today. They lived and loved and lost. Remembering that makes me feel much less alone.

After sixteen years in San Francisco, I've stored up about a gig and a half of brain space on what this city used to look like before it was destroyed by the earthquake and fire of 1906. I almost time traveled once: I'd spent a couple of hours in the history room at the library studying pre-disaster photographs. When I got back out onto the very same street I'd been studying, the "then" and "now" tried to occupy my brain at the same time for a split second, and it made my mind reel.

Meanwhile, back in the 1940s, right here in America we lived on rations. You couldn't buy anything without government coupons. You couldn't drive over 35 mph; all extra tin and metal was collected for the war effort. (Kinda puts the ban on poppers into perspective, doesn't it?) I'm told when my grandmother's last pair of nylons got ripped, she just sat down and cried. It would be years before she'd see another pair.

Trivial? History made my grandmother cry; one of the strongest people I ever knew.

Is it a useless factoid that I'm now the age my parents were when they got divorced with three teenaged kids? I don't know how they got through it without vomiting.

In England, in 1900, over four thousand people died in laundry related accidents that year alone.

So now it *is* 2006. Life in this country these days has gotten too surreal lately. I'm not a fan.

They used to worry about the Black Plague, religious intolerance, and threats of imminent attack.

Now, we worry about the Bird Plague, religious intolerance, and threats of imminent attack. And there's always someone saying things'll get worse.

So I drown in history a little. Not to make myself feel bad, but to remember we're all in this planet thing together. The connectivity helps.

Things are pretty good here and now. Few of us are ripped from our beds and shot in the street. We don't actually have the Spanish Inquisition in San Bernardino County, although if we don't pay attention, we certainly could.

Pick an era. Learn some trivia if nothing else. Put yourself there. Play. It's imagination and learning all rolled into one.

For a fun and easy glimpse of what I'm talking about, pick up and read *Time and Again* by Jack Finney. Failing that, if you're really ass-lazy, just watch *Back to the Future* on TBS again. 1985 is a bygone age itself.

Luke

GSA Precursor: Student Homophile League

Since you are reading this article, dear discriminating reader, I expect you recognize the Gay-Straight Alliance concept practiced in many high schools today. Understandably, you may believe the GSA movement the first widespread efforts in education regarding sexual orientation. Of course, your friendly gay historian must pop your balloon yet again. Bet you didn't know that a small student-driven organization began influencing American educators regarding this issue over four decades ago!

Robert Anthony Martin, Jr. (under the movement pseudonym "Stephen Donaldson") was born in Norfolk, Virginia on July 27, 1946. After briefly moving to Florida in 1965, when Donaldson's mother discovered his intimate relationship with a Cubano there, she threatened to expose his homosexuality to his father and to Columbia University, where Donaldson intended to begin school that fall. *Gay Power* (2006) relates, "Assuming that his father would cut off financial support and that Columbia would refuse to enroll him, [Donaldson] ran away to New York City. There, [he] soon encountered … several leading members of [early gay rights organization] the Mattachine Society, including Frank Kameny …."

But the story really begins (as so many American gay history stories begin) with Frank Kameny. With others, Kameny founded Washington, D.C.'s Mattachine Society in 1961, and still serves as the movement's most consistent (and arguably most effective) dynamo. Kameny told me in 1993 that Donaldson "spent the summers of '66 and '67 [with me] as a house guest. ... And sort of also took me as kind of a mentor."

Exposure to Kameny and his bold ideas likely radicalized Donaldson. Perhaps as a result, Donaldson gambled that Columbia might enroll him as the nation's first openly gay student. *Gay Power* reports that, after much internal debate, Columbia did enroll Donaldson for the 1965-66 school year: he "understood he was 'a precedent case'; he was 'the first officially recognized homosexual student to be tolerated.'" Donaldson endured a difficult first year: "To his great frustration, he could not find any other gay students or faculty members. He began the year living with three other students in a dorm suite, but ... they felt uncomfortable living with a homosexual. The dean relocated [Donaldson] to a single room in another dorm. 'This traumatic event,' he later wrote, 'was largely responsible for motivating me to form SHL.'"

According to *The Encyclopedia of Homosexuality* ("*EOH*"), "Returning to the campus as a bisexually-identified sophomore in September 1966, Donaldson discussed the idea [of a gay campus group] with interested students and, finding resistance within New York Mattachine to an autonomous group on campus, he chose the name Student Homophile League (SHL)." SHL held its first formal meeting on October 28, 1966.

As *EOH* continues, "The incipient group, which mixed both gender and orientation, found a protector in the courageous Episcopal Chaplain of the University, John Dyson Cannon. In October 1966 [Cannon] arranged a meeting [at which] a certain amount of opposition was voiced, and to gain official standing the group was required to submit a list of names of members to the university administration—which could have been ordered to disclose them to the government. This proved an insuperable barrier until a set of prominent student leaders agreed to become the official charter members [on April 19, 1967]. With this list in hand, the university capitulated ...." *Gay Power* concludes, "SHL became the first gay student group to be officially recognized by an American university administration and quickly evolved into the first gay liberation organization in the United States."

EOH reports, "The student movement spread quickly and contributed a major impetus, first to the spread of militancy and later to the radicalization of the homophile movement. ... The newly recognized [SHL] was primarily interested in educating the campus, in promoting gay rights, and in counseling. ... Many students still in the process of 'coming out' needed peer counseling, while frequent, informal discussions in the dormitories had the aim of enlightening the rest of the student body."

As Liz Highleyman wrote in her 2004 column "Past Out," "Other SHL chapters soon formed at other colleges. Women's movement pioneer and *Rubyfruit Jungle* author Rita Mae Brown started a chapter at New York University [in 1967]. In 1968, chapters were created at Stanford and Cornell."

According to *EOH*, "By the spring of 1969 the gay student organizations were beginning to integrate school dances and sponsor their own, while their ideological positions, originally heavily influenced by Kameny through Donaldson, who broke away in 1968, became even more assertive in enunciating ... 'gay liberation' doctrines. ... [S]tudent groups multiplied across the country, and by the end of the 1970s virtually every major campus in the country had one."

Robert Martin/Stephen Donaldson graduated from Columbia in 1970. After an eclectic life, Donaldson died on July 18 or 19, 1996 in New York City (allegedly from AIDS). Time and (word) space forbid me from discussing Donaldson's later noteworthy exploits. Suffice it to say that, like so many in the GLBT movement before and after him, he lived and died a controversial character.

As for Columbia's SHL? According to an LGBT encyclopedia, "After several more years of SHL campus activism, Columbia's administration established in 1971—in the basement of Furnald Hall – the 'Furnald Gay Lounge,' today called the 'Steven [sic] Donaldson Queer Lounge,' and instituted the First Friday Dance, a monthly event that [continues] to this day ...." Today, according to its website, the Columbia Queer Alliance, SHL's predecessor, "seeks to keep in time with the changing needs of our community, and we stand as heralds for the representation and protection of the LGBTQ community at this world-class university." But perhaps Wayne Dynes, in *Before Stonewall* (2002), summarizes this saga best: "When all is said and done, however, only a person of exceptional dedication and imagination [*i.e.*, Donaldson] could have founded Columbia's [SHL], a first ... that has happily produced many thorns in the sides of stiff college administrators and tight-assed alums everywhere."

Paul

Gel Us

I sure as hell get jealous. Still. After nearly two decades being a single man in the gay Sin City of San Francisco, I always get my feelings hurt by all the fucking around.

I hate it.

You may be wondering to yourself, "How can a single person be jealous? Don't you need, like, perhaps, a partner in order to have someone to be jealous of?"

Ah-SO desu-né. Traditionally speaking, you'd be correct. That one little realization took me over ten years to make, and even then I can't always calm myself down and just enjoy the sleep of a slut.

I know if I'm not in an actual promised relationship with a guy, it's none of my business that he's still fucking other people, right? Except that he is still fucking other people. And he'll tell me about it. And my feelings will get hurt because maybe I like him, and I can only smile through gritted teeth and remain silent.

Ayup. I've got one hell of a mental mess on my hands. I've come to peace with the fact that I will never do well in the Critical Mass of bear events. I stay away from big Lazy Rendezvouses and I.B.Grrs ... because I always find myself going boo hoo in the corner, away from the rivalry and sport fucking and trophy trickery. For beneath all that fun is a layer of callousness and competition that, in my head and heart, turns the beauty of sex into something akin to a weapon.

Instead, I'll stay home and cruise for dick on Craigslist. That way I can control what I see and hear. And I won't get my wires crossed—I won't like a guy only to have to watch him make out with other people in the lobby, or be a notch on his belt, compared openly with the other notches.

The one thing that makes our gay culture so fun and wonderful at the same time makes it ghoulish and evil. We have so much sex! Guys are going to keep fucking out there— which is good. I'd like to be one of the ones having the sex, yes please, very much. But in those cases when I'm not, either by profound ugliness or bad timing, or because he moves on to someone else, I get jealous.

It's very childish, really. I hate this about myself.

If someone eats pumpkin pie in front of me I don't get jealous because I don't get a piece of pumpkin pie. I've even been fairly gracious around all the iPhone users out there, knowing I can't possibly afford one of my own right now.

But dangle a man who I happen to like in front of me and invite me to sniff your finger .... I just shut the hell down. Smack my ass and call me Sally.

I think it's precisely because I haven't had a stable, secure relationship in over eighteen years—not even so much as a boyfriend—that I react this way. Nearly every time I unzip a guy's fly, I wonder, on some basic level, if he could be "The One." Usually he's not the one, and I know it instantly, such as when he has an obnoxious personality, or, worse, a way small dick. But I'm still looking. Which means that I'm carrying a lot of baggage to even the most fleeing sexual encounter.

Who doesn't love to encounter baggage in a trick!

I love sex so much that I get offended when people treat it all callous and get mean. Of course, I've occasionally succumbed to being callous myself, having once or twice pointed a finger and snickered with my friends at someone who was So Bad in Bed that it defied even the possibility of human reproduction. But if someone is just plain mean about all the fucking they do; or if he consistently blabs and has no feelings; or if I kinda like him but I can tell he's inelegant about getting his freak on, then I'll avoid him.

I guess I'm still just looking for a safe space out there.

Yet there really isn't a safe space. Guys are going to keep fucking. And they're apparently not going to be silent about it, either. So what does a person do to not get hurt?

I don't have a magic answer here, but I sense "shut up and get over it" will feature prominently. People who whine about the behaviors of others are such a pain in the ass! And here, apparently, I'm one of them.

Say I do get a boyfriend: I'll get to go through the joy of learning who's already had him. For you know they will be legion in number, and all with tales to tell, blurting out things like, "Well, I hope you have better luck with his snoring than I did."

I constantly ask couples how they work the jealousy thing between them. The variety of rules and techniques is really quite amazing. Some couples truly remain monogamous. Some couples truly don't give a shit. Most couples fall somewhere in the middle, working hard to protect the feelings of their partners. Or to at least make sure he doesn't find out about it.

Every once in a while, a coupled guy will tell me a beautiful thing: That he loves his partner so much that seeing him get his rocks off with another man actually makes him happy, for he's getting what he wants and he loves him.

Aren't people full of shit?

Truthfully, I don't think monogamy would work for me in a gay relationship—which actually just adds fuel to the fires of loneliness in my otherwise fabulous life. So I keep hidden from the possibilities of luvv, mostly just because I'm scared.

I'm looking pretty goddamned messy to you right now. Way T.M.I. I can promise you that in most other respects I'm a very balanced and healthy person.

Just this one powder keg of crap gets in my way time and time again.

So I write it all before you, warts and all. Looking for answers and, more importantly, hoping I'm not the only gay guy out there who wants to find a little sweetness among the cockrings and gloryholes.

Guys're all going to keep fucking.

I hope to be one of them.

Luke

American Trans Pioneer: Christine Jorgensen

Transgender issues have certainly become the "new frontier" in the LGBT community over the last decade or so, garnering considerably more attention and publicity. Let's re-visit the most visible American trans pioneer, who found the courage to align her physical sex to her mental sex more than half a century ago. Society's understanding has grown more sophisticated in some ways since those long-ago days, yet in other respects we continue to display a galling ignorance toward those who deviate from "the norm."

Born May 30, 1926, George William Jorgensen, Jr. wasn't like other little boys—and apparently never wanted to be. In a February 15, 1953 interview for *American Weekly*, Christine related,

> I never grew to be as husky as other little boys in the community and, as early as I can remember, I wondered why I had to wear clothes so different from my sister Dorothy's pretty dresses. I hated boys' suits and I hated little boys for their rough-and-tumble games, which I never joined, and for the questioning look I always seemed to see in their eyes. "Sissy, sissy," they would call after me ....

(Punishment and social disapprobation toward those exhibiting gender nonconformity in the U.S. remain issues today, if perhaps not quite as extreme as they were seventy-five years ago.)

So this slight, feminized lad must have been a latent homosexual, right? George didn't think so: In Christine Jorgensen's 1967 autobiography (reprinted in 2000 with an introduction by historian Susan Stryker), she revealed her emotional difficulty upon finding herself attracted to an older male friend:

> During the months in service, I had seen a few practicing homosexuals, those whom the other men called "queer." I couldn't condemn them, but I also knew that I certainly couldn't become like them. It was a thing deeply alien to my religious attitudes and the highly magnified and immature moralistic views that I entertained at the time. Furthermore, I had seen enough to know that homosexuality brought with it a social segregation and ostracism that I couldn't add to my own deep feeling of not belonging.

(I sense that many people have found—and continue to find—themselves on the horns of such a dilemma, trying to determine how to adapt themselves to binary systems (i.e., male/female; homo/hetero) that don't fit their particular situation, and that carry with them certain weighted expectations of behavior and ethics. Today we may better understand that attempting to squeeze one's self into a binary category (in a non-binary world) virtually guarantees unhappiness and personal unfulfillment.)

In 1950, Jorgensen bravely migrated to Scandinavia, intending doctors to perform a rudimentary sex-change operation that would change "him" into "her." Endocrinologist Dr. Christian Hamburger and his surgical team performed their first operation on Jorgensen in Copenhagen, Denmark, on September 24, 1951 (removing his testicles), and then a second surgery detaching his penis in November 1952. While recuperating from the second surgery, an acquaintance allegedly leaked information about Jorgensen's medical procedure to the *New York Daily News*. On December 1, 1952, the *News* ran the eye-popping headline, "Ex-GI Becomes Blonde Beauty: Operations Transform Bronx Youth." While not the world's first sex-change operation, it became the first to capture the American public's attention. Christine (who chose her post-transition name to honor Dr. Hamburger) hoped to settle into obscurity. Instead, she suddenly discovered an American media poised to devour her story and regurgitate it to an eager audience.

(Of course, American society has developed far more sophistication about transgender issues; our days of morbid curiosity regarding this topic lay forever behind us. Unless you are Gwen Araujo or Brandon Teena (or countless others), killed by young men who fear and hate gender nonconformity upon their discovering your perceived "ruse" of cross-dressing.)

Upon Christine's return to the United States on February 13, 1953, she struggled to find employment. She lamented in *American Weekly*,

> "None of the telegrams ask if I have any talent," I told my friends when my sense of humor returned, "but they all want me to perform. My musical ability and my singing voice are not of Metropolitan caliber, as you all very kindly have informed me, so what do they expect me to do, appear in local nightclubs wearing ostrich feathers?"

Denied other opportunities, and to satisfy a curious public, Christine ultimately mounted the stage. She learned to sing and dance and act (sort of), and traveled around the world, entertaining audiences for years. Jorgensen's autobiography disarmingly describes her theatrical experiences (and audience, management, and critical reaction to it and to her):

I'd been courted, derided, admired, made the subject of off-color jokes, and clothed in the light of half-truths and controversy. Apparently there would be no attitudes in between complete hostility and total approval. I was going to be like eggplant — one either liked it very much, or not at all.

(Underemployment and unemployment remain serious issues for many transgender people today. Look at Steve/ Susan Stanton, fired from her job earlier this year as City Manager of Largo, Florida because she intended to transition. Or consider the plight of others, refused secular employment, who find themselves forced by necessity to work in the sex trade.)

While Jorgensen dated men, and allegedly became engaged twice, she never married. After a long career, Christine Jorgensen died from bladder and lung cancer in San Clemente, California on May 3, 1989.

Stryker succinctly eulogized Jorgensen: "She threw herself heart and soul into playing the part of the world's first famous transsexual: educating and entertaining, being gracious and glamorous, striving for the respect that every individual should be given as a birthright, but which is all too often denied those—like Jorgensen—who express their gender identity in an atypical fashion. ... Given a very narrow path to walk through life, she found a way to walk it with style. This act of simple dignity is her enduring achievement and greatest legacy."

Paul

Internetually Speaking

My name is Luke, and I am an internet addict.

"Hi, Luke!"

My earliest internet experiences were through Compu-Serve on a 2400 baud telephone modem and $3,000 black and white Apple PowerBook. Even at such a tender young age, back in 1992, I quickly learned that I could cruise for dick on the bulletin boards. And my life was complete. For I could live out my fondest dreams while in bed with my feet up and the TV on.

God saw it, and it was good.

Back in the day, downloading one tiny B/W photo of my next husband would take twenty minutes. My family under-stood that if my phone line was busy then I was "on the computer." Even now, in the age of broadband wireless, my mom still tells my voicemail "you must be on the computer ,,,."

I met some good people. I met some real trainwrecks. My brain never had to work very hard, and my hypothalamus was constantly erect.

Going online is the first thing I do in the morning with my coffee; it's the last thing I do at night before bed. And you do the exact same damn thing. Don't lie to me.

For years, my primary goal—besides an excuse to stay indoors—was to look for some ass and Amanda Hugg. That'll never change; in fact, if I ever *get* my own man, what would I do about all the internet time/gestalt/thingy I've got invested?

But I'm older now. Friends have become much more important. All my friends are on the internet, too. It's a new type of friendship. Not all bad.

First, though, let's talk about how *weird* people get online! Gawd. Damn. Even striking up a basic cyber friendship isn't easy. They fall in love with you even though they've never met you and they live 3,000 miles away; they get pissy when you don't love them back; they feel empowered and important when they're actually just hiding behind glass and wires.

You'll agree with me, I'm sure, that the Flake Factor is immense: Whether for friendship or sex, people drop the ball and rarely actually come out from behind their computers to meet you in real life. All contact remains fleeting and tentative. Even after you've seen each other in "meatspace." People don't show up.

It will always remain much easier to stay home with your feet up and wait for something better.

When it comes to hooking up for sex, we all know the term "AOL Inches": If a guy says he's got eight inches of dick online, you better be happy with five. If he says he's forty-eight years old, he'll really be fifty-six; and 220 pounds means he's pushing 290 and succumbing to gravity like Huckleberry Hound on a hot day. (Which is fine—I'm not impugning the body style, just the online presentation. Honest.) Men who declare themselves to be total bottoms seem to adore luring us in with pictures of their huge floppy dick, proving once again, "The bigger the meat, the higher the feet." Or the ones—I love these—they show a pulsating, dripping dick (or worse), and claim they're only looking for quiet friendships and walks on the beach.

"Chat me up ... will respond to all." Well, not to YOU. Ick. You're gross.

No matter how long you chat with a guy or how good his pictures are, you simply don't know if you're a match until he opens the door. They are always different than you imagined. Sometimes better. Sometimes not.

'Twas this very mechanism that allowed me, late one rainy Valentine's Night, to motorcycle across town to do a stranger — only when I put my finger to the buzzer, it was my (recently) ex-therapist. I'd seen his picture online; he'd seen mine. But we didn't make the connection until I read the name on his door, and no, I did not ring the bell nor go inside. I'm sure even therapists need to get their dicks sucked, but I fail to see why it should be my responsibility to do so.

Amazing things have come my way because of the internet. Not just the online banking and DMV transactions, but real, substantive, life-altering events. Because of the internet I managed to buy a house in San Francisco during the height of the housing crunch. I went to meet an artist from online at his studio who then had to take cookies out of the oven. I followed him to his kitchen and saw a hidden abandoned cottage that I ultimately managed to bring back to life. I owe it all to the internet. And to cookies.

It's on account of the internet that I have my current doctor, therapist (female, this time), and accountant. And every day I look at www.stuffonmycat.com — without which life wouldn't be worth living.

When our friend died of cancer last year, an outpouring of support, cards, flowers, teddy bears, and PayPal cash flowed in via the internet. Jaw-dropping gifts and concern from people who had never met Jeff, or who only knew him online. (Cremation costs $1,800. When the funeral people turned to Jeff's mom and said, "So, you wanna just write us a check?" she nearly slid to the floor in defeat. But the bears on the broadband had chipped in money for a total stranger. It all came out OK.)

So it's a community, there in those little boxes. Everyone has a voice, even those who maybe we wish wouldn't. Me, I'm raising chickens now in my cottage. They have their own webpage, and people I don't even know come up to me and start asking after Noodle and Pecky.

How much is *too* much time on the internet? How much of it is false? To each his or her own decision, of course. When the internet leads to real life interaction, it's good. When it blocks real life interaction—it's even better.

Hello to all you wonderful people out there in the dark.

I've got a really, really big dick.

Luke

Sex and Politics

Sex sells. Jack sells sex. Jack does well. Jack does good.

That, in a nutshell, describes the life of Jack Campbell, one of my favorite entrepreneurs. In 1965, Jack began the Club Baths in Cleveland, Ohio; his Club Bath Chain became the world's largest bathhouse network. Campbell has thus earned his living for over forty years now. But Jack has never received sufficient credit for his long, generous philanthropic record—both personally and financially—to the gay community. (I believe I am the only gay historian to talk with Campbell at length about his movement activities, as I profiled him in *Leading the Parade*.)

After moving to Florida in 1972, Campbell followed in several of his relatives' political footsteps in 1975 by running for State Commissioner, finishing second in a four-person race. In *And the Band Played On*, gay journalist Randy Shilts wrote, "Without dispute, [Campbell] was the most powerful gay leader in Florida." But in 1977, Campbell (and the country) would face a stiff challenge.

In the 1970s, America's gay community began making significant political advances, as several jurisdictions abolished archaic sodomy laws and instituted civil rights protections. Toward that end, in 1976 Campbell co-founded the Dade County Commission for the Humanistic Rights of Gays "here in my home. ... There were people from the [Metropolitan

Community] Church. There were people from the Thebans Motorcycle Club. It was quite a mixed group of gays, and we endorsed candidates." DCCHRG quickly achieved success: Campbell modestly related, "We were extremely lucky—I think 76% of the candidates we endorsed won."

One candidate, newly-elected Dade County Commissioner Ruth Shack, introduced a bill to prohibit discrimination against gays and lesbians in employment, housing, and public accommodations; on January 18, 1977, the Commission approved the bill 5-3. However, that decision inflamed singer/ second-runner-up to Miss America/orange juice pitchwoman Anita Bryant (Shack's husband served as Bryant's manager). Bryant asserted that gay teachers would attempt to prosely-tize her children into the "homosexual lifestyle" (as if!), but she became an unwitting (witless?) pawn for what devel-oped into the Religious Right to attack lesbians and gays in the name of God. (Campbell, for one, acknowledged the purity of Bryant's intentions, telling a *Newsweek* reporter, "A lot of people think she's doing this for publicity, but I don't doubt her sincerity or her motives for a moment. I know how Baptists think. There's just this feeling that homosexuals are not God's chosen people.")

Despite DCCHRG's success, because "we didn't have any gays here who knew anything about politics," Jack turned to experienced New Yorkers and Californians (who later faced accusations of "carpetbagging") in an attempt to counter the looming referendum. That campaign proved unsuccessful, as on June 7, 1977, Dade County voters reversed the Commission's decision by a greater than 2:1 margin. That evening Campbell told a crowd at Miami Beach's Fontainebleau Hotel, "While we are all saddened by losing what has been a hard-fought political campaign fraught with confusion, distortion, and myths, there is much that we have achieved .... Our ultimate victory in achieving Constitutional and human rights is simply a matter of time." Unfortunately, the Miami defeat began a seventeen-month siege, as voters in St. Paul, Minnesota, Wichita, Kansas, and Eugene, Oregon similarly revoked legal protections for gay people.

(Only after the Dade referendum passed would Campbell learn that the Shacks knew that "Anita had had an affair [with another man] while they were in a production in New York City years ago," and that Bryant's husband, Bob Green, "was known to have homosexual activities. He didn't do it here [Miami], but he was well known up in central Florida." Hypocrisy run amok – Sen. Larry Craig, anyone?)

But the ominous cloud that thwarted gay rights in many parts of the country concealed a silver lining, as Campbell recalled: "I think the biggest thing that came out of it was the unification of the gay community — not only here, but across the country. ... Fortunately, when the State of California came to their election night [November 6, 1978], it was a different story." That day, California voters rejected Proposition 6 (designed to forbid public school teachers from "advocating, imposing, encouraging or promoting of private or public homosexual activity directed at, or likely to come to the attention of, school children and/or other [school] employees") and Seattle, Washington voters rejected Initiative 13 (intending to repeal gay civil rights similar to those overturned in Dade County the year before), snapping the string of morale-sapping political defeats. Campbell accurately recognized that the common enemy galvanized lesbians and gays into action as never before—and arguably never since. (Miami Dade County Commissioners reinstated anti-gay discrimination protections in 1998; they survived an unsuccessful 2002 referendum attempt.)

Liberal lesbian leader Ginny Apuzzo shared with me, "Jack's a wonderful guy. He has been a consistent supporter of virtually every idea that has been generated on behalf of the community's interest. I genuinely believe that Jack loves this community. I think it's his first and most certainly lasting love. ... I have never seen Jack get bad-tempered, or carry a grudge, or put toxins into the mix about people." Wunderkind gay politico Steve Endean wrote in his autobiography, "When the AIDS crisis came along, Jack's connection to the recreational and impersonal sex that often happened at the baths led some activists to trash him .... These Johnny-come-lately activists were still wet behind the ears and had no idea what Jack had done. ... [A]ttacks by gay activists must have been very painful to Jack, but I never heard him complain and saw no signs of him pulling back from a movement which too often seemed prone to hateful attacks on its own." Even über-conservative gay Sgt. Leonard Matlovich recognized Campbell's often unheralded virtues, relating in his biography that Campbell "has given selflessly to the movement without ever asking for anything in return. Everything he earned in the bathhouses he has repaid a hundred fold back to the community."

Paul

Man

Men—real, straight ones—are so cool. Pretty, pretty beings. Especially cuzz they don't know anybody's looking at them. Men, as observed in the wild, have a bearing and look that makes the world a wondrous place.

Last week I drove from San Francisco to Seattle in my faggy little red car with a "Republicans for Voldemort" bumper sticker on it, then I drove inland to central Washington State to spend time with my family.

Didn't see a homosexual for days.

Being locked into the family role, out in rural America, has an effect on me. I get quietly and unrelentingly horny. Which might sound slightly sicko given the proximity of family members and all, but I think it's natural. It's a mental pressure valve. Escapism. I take a lot of naps and dream and twitch and feel the possibilities grow within my spirit. It wasn't nearly as chilly as you would think if you'd seen me, blanket wrapped over my midsection during each and every nap.

So many straight men out there in normal America! Stroller daddies, truckers, cowboys, middle-aged men in midlife crisis with receding hairlines and flabby butts that would quiver like Jell-O were I to spank them as they so richly needed to be spanked, *muchachos Méxicanos quien tiene piel oscura y bigotes grandes*. Bikers and farmers and UPS men.

I even got to see the top of a young, goateed, freckled construction worker's ass crack as he bent over in jeans and leather tool belt to fix a bit of caulk.

Felt a stirring in MY caulk. If you know what I mean.

A real hot guy works in our Castro grocery store here in San Francisco. Truth be told, he's perhaps a bit plain looking. But he's got a thing going on that drives me (and many of my neighbors) wild. Why? Cuzz he's straight—I asked his gay co-worker. Straight and narrow. If he were just another gay guy, he probably wouldn't cause this palpable reaction in my friends and me. We'd just see yet one more fairly sweet, rather plain homosexual with chapped lips and delightfully rough-looking hands. (Actually, if he were gay, he wouldn't have rough-looking hands at all. He'd moisturize.)

But he's straight. He's magic. We all swoon, try to get in his checkout line.

Making a road stop at a 7-11 in Wenatchee, Washington with my family, we encountered some good old bubbas in there, most notably a fuckin' hot construction worker who was squirting out that melted fake cheese on his nachos just as I was. I said something innocuous to him about cheese that dribbles out of a machine, to which he said nothing in return. When we got back in the car, my sister asked if I didn't ever feel threatened in places like that.

Wull. First of all, do I not present as so masculinely butch and straight that they wouldn't even notice? Tsk.

But no, I don't feel threatened in places like that. If any such bubbas gave me crap, one look into their eyes would tell them many disturbing things. They'd sense that I know way more about them than they (or even their wives) do. They'll suddenly suspect that I've already completely sussed out the hair patterns and dick size under their clothes. That I've wiped the dirty, postcoital butt of far greater than they. And that I've had all the sex they never will in their straight little lives.

Gay guys win, hands (and trousers) down. I'm convinced of it. And I think the breeders sense this, and they stay the hell away.

Now. Let us begin the topic of bagging straight men.

I'd do it all the time, if I could. And if I were callous enough. For I do think you have to be a little bit mean to pull it off.

I hit nearly every rest area on the Interstate 5 corridor for eight hunnert miles. (I pee a lot.) While I'm sure the rest stop gay-on-straight blowjob does happen—and happen frequently—I rather think the queens are telling tales out of school. I saw no evidence of how you could do it and not get caught by a six-year-old who's just tumbled out of a Toyota Sienna.

And half the truckers seem to be women these days.

But yeah, I'd love to be the kind of guy who can go land straight men and real truckers and stroller daddies. I'd smother my face in their hairy straight taboo asscheeks, and keep as much of their sperm out of the reproductive stream as I possibly could. I just don't have the guts. And when I say "callous" and "mean," I think it does take a certain amount of ... disregard ... for the comfort levels of straight men to go hitting on them. I don't quite hate them enough to casually blow their whole conception of life.

Yes, I said "blow." And you smiled.

Slut.

But gimme a chance, let a straight guy come to me ... and I REPRESENT!

I've had a few. I told you this story before in a previous column (and I'll repeat it every chance I get!) about a straight guy just out of prison who told me he'd been tweaking on crystal meth, and wanted to take it up the ass from a gay man. You're saying he was gay as a fresh spring morning, right? But no. Even though I had his ankles on my shoulders for more than a few minutes, he was still straight. That feeling—that differentness to him—never went away.

(And say no to drugs!)

What is it about straight bubbae? How can we so palpably detect them, even from a great distance? They wear different clothes. I mean, I doubt breeders wear half as much Carhartt and Cabelas as we do.

Heterosexual men exude a certain essence. We love them because they're masculine, powerful, pure, like our fathers ... and because we know for sure they'll never follow us home after we suck them off.

Bask in the presence of a construction worker. A cowboy. Enjoy the goatee on the man in the Lexus one lane over.

And if you can, finger a few.

Just don't be mean to 'em, OK?

Luke

Cris and Tret

While I write this column in cold November, it won't see light of day until Valentine's Day. All the other columnists are likely telling "happy" love stories. (Nothing wrong with that—I, luckily, live one every day.) But I relate here a more cautious tale about a passionate love story that went sadly awry. (Note: Despite traditional journalistic standards, I report only one side of this saga here, having interviewed only one party involved.)

I interviewed Cris Williamson in September 2003, not long after her iconic lesbian relationship collapsed. Cris and guitarist/singer/sound engineer Tret Fure met on May 15, 1980, as Fure engineered Williamson's album *Lumiere*. Williamson told Laura Post in *Backstage Pass*, "Suddenly, everything fell into place. My whole personal life and my career. Tret had the keys to all the rooms and information about which I had minimal knowledge, the language of the studios." (Cris further told me that Tret "was pretty. She was real androgynous. Looked like Jackson Browne. Had that same look that he had, that pretty-boy. ... She dressed like a boy, and she did boys' work.") Sparks flew; lightning sizzled—select any appropriate metaphor. Quickly, the two women fell in love, becoming lovers for nearly two decades. Williamson even revealed to Diane Anderson in an October 1997 *Girlfriends* article that she and Fure "are the poster children for codependency. ... I miss her when she goes to the post office."

However, a perplexing, paradoxical problem festered beneath the seemingly flawless veneer, although Cris identified it only retrospectively with me: The relationship

was perfect, for me. Because it was *my* dream. I made my dream come true. You know, I could find the perfect person who could do all of the technical shit. Handle all that, including the money, the math—great math skills. I have none. We can write together; we can live together; we'll travel together. We built a house together. And at the end of it, I realized, a lot of it, I'd probably forgotten to ask her what her dream was. Just really fit her into my dream, and made that come true. But I think I forgot to ask her. As we often do.

Fure's attention—and affections—began wandering. On New Year's Day 2000, Cris steeled herself to ask Tret if she was having an affair; Tret was, but couldn't bring herself to tell Cris:

So I asked the question; I did the discovery. ... We were at her family's place, where we went every New Year's. Big blizzard; big whiteout going on up there. ... So I just jumped into my ski clothes, [and] walked out into a blizzard all day. And literally, a couple of times, I just fell to my knees in the snow, and said, you know, "Help me! Deliver me!" And honestly, the voices would just come, you know—"We don't deliver!" ... And when Tret and I broke up, I—I broke. Shattered. I ate glass for a year. Daily, like a ritual. And crawled through it. On hands and knees. 'Cause I was struck low. ... Hit right 'twixt the eyes with a big hammer. Brought to my knees. Humbled. Everything that a great death does to you. It rained down all around my ears. I didn't know if I was going to live. I just begged for my heart to stop. ... She was my drug. And I just loved her so.

The breakup damned near killed Williamson. As she told me, the despair brought her "right up to the edge of Lake Superior. And I heard the voices. And I said, 'Just a couple of steps more.' And I'm thinking of my girl, Sylvia Plath. And I'm thinking Anne Sexton. And Virginia [Woolf]. The girls [all writers; all suicides] are all right here on my shoulders." Fortunately, Cris turned back. But such is the devastating power of love gone astray.

And fortunately for the rest of us, Williamson crystallized her experience into a truly gorgeous CD, 2001's *Ashes*. (I'm surprised I haven't melted its grooves yet; she and gay male artist Mark Weigle speak to me musically unlike anyone else.) Williamson described *Ashes* to me as "songs from the wound. I just literally pulled open the wound, the heart, and out it poured. It was an outpouring—aah! It was the most amazing thing. And all along, I'm just as sad as a girl can be. I'm broken-hearted. I'm dying. And the other part's going, 'This is fabulous stuff!'" And Williamson deserves a Purple Heart (or maybe Indigo; some shade of deep blue) for emotional bravery, telling me, "As soon as I could stand upright, I came right out on stage with [my pain]. And I could see people go, [Gasps]. It's so hard to walk out. I went, 'Look, I know it's hard for you. If I can take it, you can take it.'" Even then, Cris retained her fabulous sense of humor: "The truth is, 'Oh, please! You can't be more sad than I am! I get to be sad first!'" On her website, Cris wrote, "My guess is these spells for grief will do their work in the world, fostering healing, nourishing others." (They did for me; I'll bet they would for you, too.)

But even I don't have a heart of stone; even this story has the requisite happy ending. After eighteen months on her own, Cris shared with me,

> I'd read the Runes, and they'd say, you know, "It looks like loss. I know it does. But opportunity opens the door! See who's there!" And, by God, it was my old friend Judy [Werle]. Who had broken up with her girlfriend. And called me for consolation. And in turning to me, for succor, for, you know, charity of feeling and advice. She freed me from my sorrow.

And they lived happily ever after (well, so far!). Happy Valentine's Day, Cris and Judy. Happy Valentine's Day, Kurt. Happy Valentine's Day to all my readers, whether partnered or single.

Paul

City Mouse

I've been thinking about giving up on San Francisco.

Not in anger or frustration, but simply because my house is eating me alive, and I don't know how much longer I want to keep struggling.

Prices are a little weird here, if you haven't heard.

Of course it gets me to thinking, as does everything else real or imagined. I wouldn't trade my 18 years of experiences here for all the zero-point interest-only mortgages in the world.

Something special happens when you have a huge gay population like here in San Francisco and in New York. There's a critical mass, an inertia, that means you can do whatever you want, do *who*ever you want, and still, hopefully, feel connected to a small, gay town feeling.

At least, that's the plan.

Gay attendance has dropped measurably here in the past two decades, for reasons of the economy and of the dying. Yet San Francisco is still a place where you can get some serious phreak on, where you don't have to actually know the person you're binking.

Comes in handy, being a bachelor for as long as I have.

Sometimes, though, I think if you want lasting friendships or, gawd-help-you, an actual lover, you're hosed in a town like this. No one wants to hear it.

By virtue of the fact that I'm an airline man, I've had the wondrous pleasure of dropping in and being a fly on the wall in most of your cities throughout the US and Canada. I've seen the hot gay men in your bars, read your gay weekly newspapers, and shopped for love over your own local internets.

Each city out there has its own feel and style and cliques and Regulation Hotties.

And one thing is certain: everybody bitches about the quality of "gay life" in their own city. The grass always seems hairier just across the border.

I grew up in Seattle, and was only just out in the gay life of Capitol Hill before settling into a closed (in more ways than one) relationship. Then I was quickly transplanted to San Francisco for a new job, on my own, with hardly time to catch my breath. My real coming out was here amid the AIDS crisis and early Bear days, when Bear meant ZZ-Top and lots of heavy-ass drugs.

Both New York and San Francisco have lost their power as gay nexuses (nexii?). What really leveled the field, I believe, has been the internet. Now New York and San Francisco are places people go for a weekend to get nasty—and, if I may speak for the general population here at least, we say thankee, sai.

But you can live just about anywhere now and still feel connected to a larger gay entity if you have a fat enough pipe.

I'm wondering if I could handle living in a place much less homo-dense than San Francisco. The idea actually scares me, not to mention how much I despise change. People I know who have left San Francisco for places like Seattle, San Diego, and Portland have expressed frustration at the change of gay pace. Some have even come back to San Francisco, and almost all of the ones who return are single. That's a very big clue, isn't it?

Relationship people seem to have community wherever they go, because it sleeps in the bed right next to them. 'Tis the single people who rattle around a bit, looking for greater meaning and connectivity.

I'm therefore very worried about where I'll end up if I have to go. I'm a West Coast guy for sure, so that means San Diego, L.A., Portland, Seattle, Vancouver, Denver, or Calgary. Oh. And the granddaddy of them all–lllliterally–Palm Springs.

I just spent a week in Palm Springs, thinking I might want to move there. It's where this very magazine is published! I know many guys who live there, and its hot desert weather appeals to this writer. But my week down there left me shivering in the heat. It's a fine place, don't get me wrong; I vacation there at least once a year. It just didn't feel right for me. It almost feels like a lot of the more hardcore element of San Francisco just packed up their drugs and boas, and now they're all down in Palm Springs, not returning phone calls.

Interestingly enough, this has turned San Francisco into a much smaller gay town, one that breathes easier now. Or maybe I've been here long enough that I know how to find my way amid the more unsavory elements, and I'm living in a fool's paradise.

Take Portland, Oregon. Please. I've been there a lot lately for work. Great town! I really like it up there. Hot men, livable city, close to my family in Seattle; and while I don't understand that hoopy new strung up gondola thing stretching over I-5 to the hospital, I'm nevertheless willing to suspend my disbelief on it.

Yet when I ran through all the profiles on the bear chat sites, I swear each and every one of them said:

"Not looking for hook-ups!"

"No quick hookups!"

"If that's all you want, then move on!"

WTF? Didn't I just see you down at IBR drinking piss out of the urinals?

It reminds me of what I often hear said about Boston, that no one ever has sex in Boston. They go to Providence and Provincetown, get their fill, come back home and lie about it.

Sigh.

I think I know the answer: in a city with fewer per capita butt pirates, everyone's going to know everyone else's business. It wouldn't take long to play the smaller field, and suddenly everyone's a sister to everyone else.

The theory is that you should be able to live anywhere and still make it all work. Finding love in a big candy store like San Francisco is possible. And so is a quick hookup in San Diego's Balboa Park.

The answer lies, as always, in being true to what you want; in communicating that need to others; in not dissing the needs *from* others; and in NEVER USING A SECOND EQUITY LINE AGAINST A NEG-AM MORTGAGE!

I'd like to thank the residents of Portland and Palm Springs and Boston for being on today's panel. Tune in next month when our guests will be Old People, and Those Who Love Them.

Luke

LGBT Youth and Suicide

I wouldn't wish my junior high school experience in California, in the 1970s, on my worst enemy. Struggling with my sexual orientation; praying daily not to "pop a boner" in the showers; suffering hazings by eighth and ninth graders. Simultaneously, my mother was telling me, "These are the best years of your life!" Retrospectively, I'm not surprised that suicide seemed a legitimate option to cope with my alienation. What about LGBT kids in an even less welcoming environment, such as Northern Nevada?

Ask Ben Felix, A Rainbow Place's founding Executive Director. In an e-mail interview, Ben shared with me,

> In December of 1999, we suffered a series of five suicides here in Washoe County due to gender/sexual identity issues. Because of fear of stigma, many families declined to acknowledge the issues surrounding the deaths. In late December, I began writing Articles of Incorporation and organizational bylaws to found a community center to provide adequate support resources for the queer community. I enlisted Bob Fulkerson, John Drakulich, Gail Faulstich—and later others—initially to review the concepts and to begin drafting a Board of Directors.

Why? Not having viable resources outside of taverns and clubs for community to gather seemed unconscionable in light of the distress that many young people were certainly experiencing. We started out by holding youth centered social activities, such as Movie & Popcorn Nights and a GaYme Night. We held a few public dances and picnics to get a routine started. We began to build our library almost immediately. We visited each faith-based community and often we were invited to speak to congregations and groups who were very positive about our mission and outreach. We networked with school counselors and began to construct a safety net for questioning or identifying youth.

According to Paul Cody, Ph.D., "Gay, lesbian, bisexual, and transgender youth (generally defined as ages 15-24) attempt suicide at a rate 2-3 times higher than their heterosexual peers. Some studies indicate that the rate of attempted suicide for transgender youth is higher than 50%. It is also estimated that gay, lesbian, and bisexual youth comprise 30% of completed suicides, with transgender youth also having a higher incidence of completed suicides." A menstuff.org article reveals, "Gay youth are up to six times more likely to attempt suicide than straight teens, and gay teenagers account for up to 30 percent of all teenage suicides in the nation. … In high-risk patients—that is, patients who have threatened or attempted suicide—there are four risk factors that account for more than 80% of the risk for suicide: major depression, bipolar disorder, a lack of previous mental health treatment, and the availability of firearms in the home. If these four problems were solved, most suicides would be prevented."

The Trevor Project's website adds: "Sexual orientation and gender identity alone are *not* risk factors for suicide. However, lesbian, gay, bisexual, transgender and questioning youth face many social factors that put them at higher risk for self-destructive behaviors, including suicide."

I spoke with Emilio Parga, founder and executive director of The Solace Tree—Child and Adolescent Center for Grief and Loss. A Pediatric Thanatologist (from Greek, "Thana" = "Death") who describes his work as "helping children prepare for funerals; I explain death to children; I'm a consultant to school districts, hospitals, and I do social work." Parga helps both children and adults grieve the loss of loved ones. I experienced him as an empathetic genuine guy with whom I would entrust my life if necessary. Himself a wounded warrior, Parga possesses an uncanny ability to listen and be present in the moment. During our conversation, we touched on several issues:

> I think this job has taught me to just listen and not point the finger or do anything that's negative because there's so much negativity and racism and bias and judgment. I think my work has really helped me to be a better person. Plus, I think I've surrounded myself at The Solace Tree with really good people. We don't stand for negativity.

> We do peer support groups for any type of death. We do them so families and kids know that they're not alone— that they can find that commonality and normalcy in their life. That's a great thing that we can offer. I ask kids, "What would you have done without The Solace Tree?" And they say, "I don't know."

I think, in their own homes, LGBT kids are breaking down the walls of silence. Whether shame or doubt, walls are being broken down. I have a feeling that, in the near future, even the middle schools may have something for them. They'll have to.

The visibility of the LGBT movement provides that young people can name and claim their sexuality earlier than I did. However, they often don't have the emotional tools to handle the potential pitfalls that accompany such a disclosure. Will they receive emotional support at home? From school friends and authorities? Specifically, what services can LGBT youth currently obtain in Reno?

To find out, I chatted with Brian Baxter, current Executive Director of A Rainbow Place:

P: You work with a lot of gay kids here. What kind of emotional health issues do you see? Are the kids more well-adjusted than we were at their ages? Do they appear to get more family support? Or peer support?

B: I don't see the family support being any stronger now than when we were their age. I do see more support for them in the schools because of the GSA (Gay-Straight Alliance) network. But I also hear from the kids that the GSAs are not getting strong support from the individual schools, and especially the adult facilitators at the schools. But I think the GSAs are very effective. These kids learn that they're not alone. When I tell kids about GSAs—just the whole general description of what a GSA is, and that they are all over the Reno area—their jaws hit the floor. "You mean I'm not the only one?"

P: That makes me think they are not reaching kids that they need to reach. They're so far underground that, unless they're plugged into a network somehow, they can't access what they need.

B: Well, for example, Galena High School has a *very* strong GSA. At Galena, these kids are *allowed* to put posters up in the hallways, at the football games, at basketball games, in the cafeteria and in the classrooms. But there are other schools where they're not allowed to post anything and it's all word-of-mouth.

P: How are the openly gay kids doing in school?

B: Quite honestly, what I've witnessed as far as graduation rates, kids dropping out, it is more often reflective of their economic situation at home. It has nothing to do with their sexual orientation.

P: The kids that you see, do they seem to have faith in their futures?

B: I'm surprised how optimistic they feel about their futures. Again, they don't know a whole lot of what they might encounter. They're not as familiar with discrimination as an adult might be, or as the people who were their age in the past might have been. It's almost like an invincibility; very empowered, but very naïve.

P: Do you have a number of trans kids who come through here as well?

B: We do. But I'm finding that the few transgender kids I see are having the exact same issues the transgender adults are having. They're afraid to come out; they don't directly identify as gay or lesbian, or bisexual. They very often feel pushed away from the LGBT community—the "T" doesn't count for anything.

P: What kinds of community organizations do these kids have to come into—you know, late teens and early twenties? Is there anything much besides the bars for them?

B: Well, there is the Half Dollar Court, under the Silver Dollar Court. It is a group that was created for youth way back when. Of course there is A Rainbow Place, and these kids can come to our structured youth group. Also, they're more than welcome to just hang out any day of the week, and just watch videos or read books in the library. There's also the Queer Student Union at University of Nevada—Reno, but I believe you probably have to be a student. The kids who aren't students at UNR, what do they do? Clearly it's a very underserved community.

When my father completed his suicide in 1982, after my mother and I had been on "death watch" for over a year (I spent my 20th birthday talking a gun out of his hand), I never seriously considered suicide again. Yet I struggled to come out fully as an openly gay man during the early days of the AIDS epidemic. At age twenty-two, I left Antioch and moved to Southern California, where I learned to access resources and began developing a "gay family of choice." Almost a quarter-century later, I have built a life for myself that others envy and that I heartily enjoy. There is life (and potentially a great one) after one's teenage years—nearly everyone struggles during that stage of life, but that battle is exacerbated for LGBT kids.

What of the future for Reno's LGBT youth? Baxter told me, "Here at A Rainbow Place, we want to set up a GSA summit so all the GSAs in the region can get together in one place. Here, they can really just bring up their own topics of what they want to discuss. Then we'll find the adults to help guide them through these things." But Brian and I expressed our frustration at the practical difficulties of implementing proactive plans:

> P: Who's going to do it; where is the money going to come from? I mean, it's all well and good to have an idea but unless you've got some money to be able to back it up—

> B: Right. Getting the heart in the right place is easy. Getting the *money* in the right place, that's impossible! [Laughs] And I'm not aware of any other game in town, especially considering that Washoe County is broke; the State of Nevada is broke; the City of Reno doesn't want to have to deal with the homeless or runaway kids.

Is this where *you* come in, caring adults? Do *you* have ideas, time, and resources? Paul Cody writes," Older gay, lesbian, bisexual and transgender people who read this can remember how difficult our own experience was when young. Frequently we may want to put that behind us because of the painfulness of remembering it even still. We cannot afford to do that. ... What will you do for those who come after us?"

Ben Felix expounded, "The sword of the term 'pedophile' hung over A Rainbow Place's founders' heads from the moment we decided to move forward with our vision. Fortunately there were many strong individuals who recognized that arcane attitudes were not going to change by themselves. These strong folks chose to turn their own experiences into something positive. I can't tell you how often I heard 'I wish I had something like this when/where I was growing up!'" More recently, Brian Baxter shared, "I know more than enough LGBT adults that are willing to help the younger generations. Otherwise we are doomed to repeat our history."

Emilio Parga told me, "The most rewarding aspect of my job is knowing that we can bring people together to know that they're not alone; that they're not going crazy; that there's someone in this world who will listen to them; who cares about them; who loves them; who will hold them; who will say, 'You're not alone.'"

If a straight man is willing to do that for our kids, aren't we? Since most LGBT folks have no biological children, can we collectively muster the will to say, "Not on my watch," and back it up with action? What better legacy can we leave for "our" kids?

Paul

Open Relationships

I never wrote a column about relationships because I've never been in one. Always the bachelor. And the reason I never had a relationship was because I knew I'd never want a closed relationship—I have oats to sow—yet was dead certain I could never handle an open relationship. The jealousy would eat me alive. Circuit: closed. Me: out.

So I stayed alone and afraid for decades.

Well I finally have a man; a good man. Going on five years now. And we're in an open relationship.

I chose him because he was hot enough, sweet enough, himself enough, that I was finally willing to lay it all on the line. I was ready to break it all open and throw myself into the fray. It hasn't been easy, and I'm not done yet. But I'm making progress. I've learned a lot.

Thus I write this column to my younger self, and to many of you out there who, like me, can't handle jealousy.

Lots of guys quite literally don't give a fuck about jealousy, and—if you're like me—you probably learned to avoid these people like the plague. They're so callous about sex that they're totally threatening to people like you and me. We're not like them. Sex and love equal the same thing. We *want* them to equal the same thing; it's very romantic, it's how all the stories play out. It's a form of Cinderella Complex, and I think it's a natural way to feel growing up: Someday I'll meet a man and fall in love, and it will be pure, and sex will only be with him, and there will be complete trust, and it will never get old.

Except ... we're gay men. We've been out having fun so long we don't know how to just shut it off and remain faithful. So we don't even try.

Well, I tried.

At first it was nearly impossible. I spent the first years (yes, *years*) in a constant state of red alert, waiting for the shock and pain of incontrovertible evidence that he's playing around.

An added little bonus is that he's gorgeous. I always wanted a gorgeous boyfriend, and now I have one: People flock to him. They come up to him in bars and stick their tongues down his throat, and here's me shrinking into the corner, ready to throw up. I quickly had to learn: Dating a gorgeous man means you'll be ignored and pushed to the side. A lot. It's up to you how you want to handle that—you can get bitter and mousy and stay in the corner, or you can speak up and make yourself heard anyway. Or at least try to. Doesn't always work.

Plus, he can flirt like no one I've ever known. He can talk a complete stranger down to his underwear in two sentences. I've seen him do it.

So you can see, I've got my work cut out for me. Not only am I prone to jealousy, I've got Rudolph Valentino on my hands, and he's not shy about it in the least.

How do I deal with it?

Well, in the first place, our relationship is "Don't Ask, Don't Tell." Which is exactly what I needed. He has given me space by putting a sock in it—I know he's out doing other guys, but he doesn't let on. He doesn't have jealousy issues himself, but he knows I do, and he's been kind enough to cover his tracks while I learn to get stronger and learn to just go with the flow. He seems to understand.

I'm the one he goes home with. We're not trying to throw any three-ways out there, and if he's clearly into some guy, I've had to learn to walk away and let them mutter their Facebook names to each other so they can find each other later. It's not my business, and I have to just be OK with that. Because I still hook up, too. Not so much anymore; that drive is dwindling away, I'd rather just get my rocks off at home. But you and I both know how validating it is to be wanted. If I love him, then I have to understand he needs validation, too.

I just don't want to see it.

The biggest lesson becomes learning the difference between sex and love. For many of us they're intertwined, and we wouldn't have it any other way. But being in an open relationship teaches you what love actually is, and it's different than I thought. The sharp pain of "I can't do this" is slowly going away as I begin to recognize this difference.

When I hook up outside the relationship, of course, I realize it's just sex—it doesn't feel threatening, it doesn't *mean* anything. It's just for fun. So naturally I have to apply the same rule to my partner. Just because he dips in the pool doesn't mean he's going to leave me. My jealousy isn't one of possession, it's one of being left out—excluded. Mocked. Left behind. I call the jealous feelings inside me the Clawer Monster, and when the Clawer Monster comes out and I get in over my head and start to feel the pangs of jealousy, I simply stop and realize two things: Sex is just sex, and tonight we'll fall asleep together curled up like puppies. Tomorrow he'll bring me coffee in bed in my favorite Hello Kitty mug. It's been *years* now. When you build that kind of closeness, the sex part starts to take on a different emphasis.

You kinda have to be there to know what I mean, and you can't be there until you're willing to put yourself on the line. It's very tricky.

I've got a long ways to go. If there's a clue left behind I'll find it, and I can't say I still don't quietly flip out a little—butterflies in my stomach, unable to eat. The first time someone came up to me and actually told me he had sex with my boyfriend "last month," you can bet I went to a pretty dark place.

"Don't Ask, Don't Tell" only works if people don't tell—and people tell. Bless their fucking little hearts.

But the pain becomes less. The dark place becomes less dark.

The land mines never go completely away. It gets messy when I find out he's been doing the same people I have, or, worse, doing someone I really want but can't have. You learn to just swing loose and be with the feelings. They're just feelings. They are information; not instructions. You don't have to *do* anything, just sit with the hurt. And suddenly you're together again, and you realize nothing has changed in your overall feelings for him. Well, maybe it's OK to be a little mad at him for a while as long as your goal is to eventually let it go. You have to let it go.

You don't have to give up on love, you just have to give up sex as being the vehicle for love.

Trust me, it won't make you a creep. It actually makes you stronger.

I always clung to my jealousy because I thought it had something to teach me. This is untrue. It can't teach anything. It's a very old, very crude defense mechanism that, as an adult, does more harm than good. It's unattractive.

Turns out that jealousy is a part of me that needs to die, and die forever. It's not easy to kill a part of yourself; it isn't going down without a fight.

But I'm going to keep on keeping on.

Obviously we're not finished. When I can face it directly, when it becomes "Do Ask, Do Tell" ... when we finally get that guy over for a three-way, and I can participate without crying, then I'll be there.

In the meantime, I don't want to rock the boat. I like things how they are, and want to keep it. I'm afraid to take it to the next level. But that day will surely come, and I know there will be hurt and fear.

The bottom line is: He's worth it. What we have together is worth it, and someday jealousy will be this thing I used to have but grew out of.

Luke

Relationships

So this is where Paul gets a little more raw.

Luke wrote his article on relationships, and I thought I should throw my two cents in.

Unlike Luke, I have been partnered more than half of my fifty-seven years – more than half of them to the same man. That doesn't make me an expert, but it does give me a very different experience from Luke's.

My husband Kurt and I also have an open relationship. Making that happen was probably the hardest thing I've ever done in my emotional life. I am not wired for monogamy. I learned it in my first relationship (gay men didn't marry back in the late 1980s), although I remain friends with my "ex" to this day—he still does our taxes! But by Kurt's and my third date (we DID date in the late 1980s!), I told him that I could not promise monogamy. Unfortunately, at that point, he didn't know me well enough to know that I mean what I say. I think he thought my saying that was like a "get out of jail free" card for me. I promised I would remain monogamous to him for a year, because I wanted him to know that my word was good. I kept my promise, and more—it was over three years after our first date before I visited the local bathhouse.

Kurt didn't like it, but he tried to accept it with good grace. I think he thought it was like a "phase." But I really crave the variety of having sex with different men. To me, it's like food—I love Mexican food, but it's not the only kind of food I like, and I wouldn't be as crazy about it if I had to eat it and nothing else every day. I told my husband, "You can't be 6'4" and dark today, and 5'5" and blond tomorrow, and it's not realistic to think you (or anyone else) are going to meet all of my sexual needs." I've never had sex with anyone who didn't want to have sex with me. I don't do it in public places. And I think this is true of a lot of married gay men—but it's a dirty little secret no one wants to talk about. (You're welcome.)

I learned from *The Male Couple* (McWhirter/Mattison, 1984) that most gay couples do not survive five years in their relationship without finding some way to accommodate extra-marital sexual relationships. Now, this was a study of male couples in the 1970s (pre-AIDS awareness) in San Diego, California—a relatively liberal place during the beginning of the sexual revolution—so it may not be true today, and may not have been true even upon its publication, as gay male sexual culture changed considerably in the early Eighties because of the threat of AIDS. Still, it seems to be true in the circles in which I travel.

I totally understand Luke's "Don't Ask, Don't Tell" stance. In fact, I expect that's how most gay male couples deal with the issue.

But I couldn't do it. To me, that would have felt like emotional cheating. I didn't (and still don't) need Kurt's permission to have sex with anyone, but I felt he had the right to know what I was doing (not a blow-by-blow, so to speak; not with graphs and charts) so he could decide how impor-tant physical monogamy was to him in our relationship. I trusted that ultimately he would be able to handle my being honest with him. I was pretty sure he wouldn't be able to handle lying and deception from me, and I knew I wouldn't be able to explain it to him after the fact and maintain any kind of personal integrity.

So from year three through year eight, we didn't fight about it, but it certainly was a source of tension in our home. We were very civilized. We negotiated rules to which we both agreed. I assured him that I wasn't leaving him, and that there was nothing "wrong" with him that he needed to fix. And what was good for the gander was good for the other gander, too—I wasn't demanding something for myself that was not reciprocal. But I expect Kurt felt exactly as Luke did—on red alert, waiting for me to tell him that I had been auditioning other lovers, that I found someone else, and that I wanted to leave him.

Gay male couples can usually negotiate this more easily than heterosexual couples (and probably lesbian couples as well) because no one is getting pregnant/birthing bastards/fighting over child support/marrying resentfully as a result of such outside relationships. And most men really enjoy sex (or at least the hunt for sex), and have the ability to separate sex from love—they intersect, but need not be contiguous.

At the end of that period—during which we engaged in a few rounds of couples therapy—Kurt became practically catatonic. I was about two days from leaving, because I was in a relationship with someone who wouldn't or couldn't talk to me. Finally, Kurt realized that he couldn't change me. He would either have to accept that this was an intrinsic part of my nature, or we would have to part ways. Of course, we are still together. (Good choice, Honey!) But I hate to think of the number of good, loving male couples who chose to separate because they couldn't be "faithful" to one another. Emotional monogamy is much more important to me than sexual monogamy—I think we do more damage to our relationships by lying to ourselves and our partners. Some sexually monogamous couples damage one another emotionally, and are jealous and resentful of one another. If that were my only option, I'd rather stay single.

Most couples fight over two things—sex and money. We have disagreed about money on occasion, but never seriously. We disagreed—strenuously—about sex for five years, and we survived it.

My advice—for what it's worth—is that you should be honest about this subject and have a frank talk about it as soon as you feel your relationship is becoming "serious." Yes, while you're "dating." If he's going to fall in love with you, then he should know exactly who he's falling in love with before either of you makes a heavy-duty emotional investment in the other. He's going to love the good things about you—duh. But can he handle your less Prince Charming-like traits? I hate the idea that you snag a guy, showing him all of your noble qualities, and then try to sneak in the bad stuff a little bit at a time once he's totally smitten with you. I know—everybody does it. Don't be like everybody. Build one solid, exceptional relationship with your soul mate.

(By the way, Luke's husband IS as drop-dead gorgeous as he describes him—at least to a bear lover like me. He also has the sweetest personality. You should just know that Luke did not exaggerate in the least.)

Paul

If you enjoyed *Bears In The Raw*, you may also enjoy
Leading the Parade by Paul D. Cain
available on <u>amazon.com</u>

www.ingramcontent.com/pod-product-compliance
Lightning Source LLC
Chambersburg PA
CBHW030515020726
47494CB00004B/1105